W9-BZR-686

Ozzy growled.

"Easy, boy," Ashley said in a low tone as she watched the headlights grow brighter. Without warning, the lights on the approaching vehicle abruptly went dark.

"Did you see that?" Ashley glanced at Chase, who nodded. "I'm taking Ozzy to check it out."

She ran across the parking lot. Had the assailant in the van come back to find Cade and the baby?

Either way, she couldn't ignore her suspicions. As she reached the road, the headlights abruptly snapped back on, blinding her with their intensity.

Then the vehicle surged toward her.

"Ozzy!" She jumped onto the sidewalk, tugging her K-9's leash. The vehicle skidded past and picked up even more speed as it disappeared around a curve in the road.

* * *

Mountain Country K-9 Unit

Laura Scott has always loved romance and read faith-based books by Grace Livingston Hill in her teenage years. She's thrilled to have been given the opportunity to retire from thirty-eight years of nursing to become a full-time author. Laura has published over thirty books for Love Inspired Suspense. She has two adult children and lives in Milwaukee, Wisconsin, with her husband of thirty-five years. Please visit Laura at laurascottbooks.com, as she loves to hear from her readers.

Books by Laura Scott

Love Inspired Suspense

Hiding in Plain Sight
Amish Holiday Vendetta
Deadly Amish Abduction
Tracked Through the Woods
Kidnapping Cold Case

Justice Seekers

Soldier's Christmas Secrets
Guarded by the Soldier
Wyoming Mountain Escape
Hiding His Holiday Witness
Rocky Mountain Standoff
Fugitive Hunt

Mountain Country K-9 Unit

Baby Protection Mission

Visit the Author Profile page at LoveInspired.com for more titles.

Baby Protection Mission

LAURA SCOTT

LOVE INSPIRED SUSPENSE
INSPIRATIONAL ROMANCE

If you purchased this book without a cover you should be aware that this book is stolen property. It was reported as "unsold and destroyed" to the publisher, and neither the author nor the publisher has received any payment for this "stripped book."

Special thanks and acknowledgment are given to Laura Scott for her contribution to the Mountain Country K-9 Unit miniseries.

LOVE INSPIRED® SUSPENSE
INSPIRATIONAL ROMANCE

ISBN-13: 978-1-335-59798-4

Recycling programs for this product may not exist in your area.

Baby Protection Mission

Copyright © 2024 by Harlequin Enterprises ULC

All rights reserved. No part of this book may be used or reproduced in any manner whatsoever without written permission except in the case of brief quotations embodied in critical articles and reviews.

This is a work of fiction. Names, characters, places and incidents are either the product of the author's imagination or are used fictitiously. Any resemblance to actual persons, living or dead, businesses, companies, events or locales is entirely coincidental.

For questions and comments about the quality of this book, please contact us at CustomerService@Harlequin.com.

® is a trademark of Harlequin Enterprises ULC.

Love Inspired
22 Adelaide St. West, 41st Floor
Toronto, Ontario M5H 4E3, Canada
www.LoveInspired.com

Printed in Lithuania

MIX
Paper | Supporting
responsible forestry
FSC® C021394

And thou shalt love the Lord thy God with all thine heart, and with all thy soul, and with all thy might.
—*Deuteronomy* 6:5

This book is dedicated to our series editor, Katie Gowrie.
Thanks for your help with these stories!

ONE

Something was wrong.

Tugging his brown cowboy hat low on his forehead, rancher Cade McNeal cradled his one-month-old nephew, Danny, to his chest as he scanned the area around him. His sister, Melissa, Danny's mother, had been acting strange lately. Jumpy, nervous and, of course, exhausted from caring for her son. She'd asked for some time alone to sleep, so he'd taken the baby with him to the store to pick up ranch supplies for the McNeal Four Ranch they'd inherited from their parents following their death six years ago. After picking up the necessary supplies, he'd lingered in town to give her extra time to sleep, buying packs of diapers, other baby supplies and some toys.

Then he'd gotten a text from Melissa asking him to meet her here, at the Elk Valley Park, nestled in the shadow of the Laramie Mountains of Wyoming. A cold March wind whipped through the air, making him cuddle the little boy closer to his chest for warmth.

He pushed the stroller with one hand, while holding Danny in the other as he searched for Melissa. Dusk had fallen, and the sky was overcast, making it seem darker than the hour of five o'clock. Danny had stopped fussing now that Cade was holding him.

Where was she? Why were they meeting here? He tried not to be annoyed with Melissa. She'd turned her life around, had been focused on being a good mother to Danny.

Danny's father, Vincent, had taken off nine months ago, wanting nothing to do with fatherhood.

Good riddance, as far as Cade was concerned.

Had his wild child sister decided to return to her old ways? Instead of resting, had she gone out to meet with someone? A guy? At twenty-two years old, she was twelve years his junior, and he could understand her wanting some sort of social life. Yet she also needed to be responsible for her son. He didn't mind helping and supporting her, but she needed to do her part, too. And, really, if she'd wanted to go out on a date, she should have asked, rather than pretend she'd needed a nap.

As his irritation grew, a figure near the far end of the parking lot caught his eye. He narrowed his gaze when a person dressed in black, complete with a black ski mask covering his face, broke into a run, heading straight toward him.

Cade instinctively took several steps backward, his brain struggling to register what was happening. Then he heard his sister's voice. "Run, Cade! Keep Danny safe! Run!"

As the masked man was gaining on him, he had little choice but to do just that. Shoving the stroller toward the guy, hoping to trip him up, Cade sprinted in the opposite direction. He was glad he was holding Danny, enabling him to move faster.

But not fast enough. Hearing the masked man's loud, heavy breathing behind him spurred him on, while he tried to avoid the worst of the icy snow-covered areas on the parking lot.

The man grabbed the collar of his thick rawhide-sheepskin coat. Holding Danny in his left arm, Cade jammed his right elbow back, hoping to dislodge the guy's grip.

When that didn't work, he jutted sideways, crossing an icy patch of ground, hoping to catch the man off guard and causing him to fall. The thug cursed when his foot slipped and he lost his grip on the rawhide coat.

"Danny!" Melissa's voice was raw with anguish.

"Stop! Police!" Another female voice reached his ears. The masked man abruptly shoved Cade forward. Now it was his turn to be caught off balance, his booted feet slipping on the snowy ground. When he felt himself falling, he twisted his body so that he fell on his right side to protect Danny.

He struggled to sit up as a woman dressed in gray slacks and a puffy black coat, accompanied by a black dog, ran toward him. Cade turned to look for the masked man in time to see him brutally shove Melissa into the open door of a dark van.

Melissa screamed, but then there was only silence as the assailant jumped in behind her and slammed the door. Whoever was driving took off.

No! Cade struggled to his feet. "Melissa!" He spun toward the female officer. "He kidnapped my sister!"

The woman was already sprinting after the van, her black Lab easily keeping pace beside her. The dog was wearing a K-9 vest, indicating they were a team. But despite her willingness to jump toward danger, her efforts were of no use. She couldn't catch the vehicle. Tires squealing, the van sped away, leaving the female officer and her K-9 partner behind.

Danny began to cry, as if sensing the danger. Or maybe from the way Cade had hit the ground, taking the brunt of the fall on his right shoulder, which throbbed painfully. As he attempted to soothe the boy, Cade grappled with the realization that his sister had been kidnapped right in front of his eyes!

And just as concerning was knowing that his one-month-old nephew was in danger, too.

* * *

Rookie K-9 officer Ashley Hanson stared at the back of the black van as it sped down the street. The license plate was covered in mud, making it impossible to get a number. She thought it might be an older model Chevy minivan but couldn't be certain in the dim light.

Turning, she ran to where the tall man wearing a knee-length brown-rawhide coat and brown Stetson stood holding a baby to his chest. The infant was dressed in a bright blue snowsuit and a pale blue hat to protect him from the cold March temperatures. Spring rarely came early to the Wyoming mountains.

"What's going on here?" She raked her gaze over him, wondering if the baby was his and if this was some sort of custody dispute.

"I believe the guy in the ski mask tried to kidnap Danny. But when you arrived, he took my sister, Melissa, instead. Danny's mother." When she still looked a bit confused, he added, "Danny is my nephew."

"Who's his father?"

"A guy named Vincent Orr. He moved out of state because he didn't want anything to do with being a father." The cowboy waved an impatient hand. "It could be he changed his mind and wanted to be involved, but then why go the kidnapping route? As the boy's father, he would have some visitation rights, no need to resort to drastic measures."

Ashley reached for the radio on her collar. There hadn't been time to call for backup, something she feared her boss would rag on her about, so she quickly did so now. "This is Officer Hanson requesting backup at the Elk Valley Park. A woman has been kidnapped and a baby was targeted, too."

"Roger that," the dispatcher's voice sounded calm even though kidnappings were a rare occurrence.

Then again, they usually didn't have unsolved homicides, either.

"You need to get cops on the road to search for that van." The tall dark-haired man's curt tone interrupted her thoughts. His green eyes pinned her with a narrow look. "Now!"

Ashley understood his concern but she also needed more information. "What is your name?"

"Cade McNeal." His voice hitched a bit as he looked down at the infant in his arms.

She had seen the man in the ski mask latch onto the collar of Cade's rawhide coat then shove him to the ground. She had been walking her K-9 partner, Ozzy, having just left a brief introductory meeting held at the Elk Valley police headquarters. A multiagency K-9 task force had been recently pulled together under federal jurisdiction to find a serial murderer they'd dubbed the Rocky Mountain Killer. He'd struck ten years ago, when three young men had been killed here in Elk Valley, but the cases had gone unsolved. Now, two recent murders, this time in two other Rocky Mountain states, had been tied to the three cold cases.

All five victims had belonged to the local Young Rancher's Club, which had been disbanded after the first three men had been found dead on a very prosperous ranch. Ten years ago, Ashley, only sixteen at the time, had known the entire police force had worked the case—only to come up empty-handed. The new victims, also previous members of the YRC, had also been found in ranchers' barns. And the fact that the 9mm slugs with the exact distinctive markings used on all five earlier victims clearly tied the ten-year-old cold case to these recent murders.

Ashley knew her task force boss, FBI special agent in charge Chase Rawlston, was not happy to have a rookie cop assigned to the team. Of course, he'd assumed she'd asked her father, Brian Hanson, head Bureau Chief in the Washington FBI office, for a favor, when in fact, she hadn't done any such thing. It still burned to know her father had insisted she be part of the team anyway. Given these murders had haunted her hometown for years, she was determined to be an asset in the case. After all, she knew many of the people living here. Hopefully, she would be able to prove herself to Chase, and to the rest of the team.

That brought her back to the current crime in progress. She glanced at Cade. "I'm Officer Ashley Hanson, and this is my K-9 partner, Ozzy. We're going to examine the crime scene. I need you and Danny to stay here to wait for my backup to arrive."

The tall rancher looked as if he'd wanted to argue, but she turned away.

"Let's get to work, Oz."

Her black Lab partner wagged his tail, excited at the prospect of going to work. For K-9s, "work" was another word for "play." Ozzy's specialty was scent tracking, but finding a victim taken by car was extremely difficult. The metal structure of the vehicle made it nearly impossible to track a scent down the road.

She headed to the area where the van had been, intently scanning the ground for any footprints. This was a park, so it wouldn't be easy to attribute one to the assailant, but she had to try. If they could find something, she'd trust Ozzy's amazing nose to take it from there.

The hard ground, icy in many places from the cold wind blowing off the mountains, didn't provide much in the way of evidence. But she kept looking since there were some areas where snow remained. Ozzy sniffed eagerly, pausing to investigate something more closely. She'd learned over the past eleven months working with him, that Ozzy didn't always have to be told to search. His instinct to pick up new and interesting scents came naturally.

Crouching next to him, she saw a partial heel print imbedded in the snow. A type of hiking boot, based on what she could see from the tread. It wasn't much, but the way the heel was dug in along the backside made her think of how the masked man had likely pushed off with his foot to get Cade's sister into the van.

"Good boy, Ozzy." She praised her partner for the find to keep him engaged. "Good boy!"

"What is it? What did you find?" She turned to see Cade and Danny hovering close. Too close.

She bit back a flash of irritation. "I'm sorry, but you need to stay back. I can't have you contaminating the crime scene."

"I apologize, that wasn't my intent. But my sister is missing," he said in a low voice. "I—we need you to find her."

"We will." She smiled reassuringly. "But please stay back, okay?"

"Yeah. Got it."

She rose and continued walking, careful to step in clear areas so as not to ruin any evidence. When she spied a black glove on the ground near the spot where the van had been, her heart thumped in her chest.

Ozzy had found it, too, sniffing the item intently. Then he'd turned and sat, looking up at her in his alert signal.

"Good boy, Oz!" She praised him again and pulled an evidence bag out of her pocket. Covering her hand with the bag, she picked up the glove, then offered the open bag to Ozzy. "This is Glove. Seek! Seek Glove."

Ozzy buried his nose in the bag, then lifted his snout to the air, sniffing eagerly. He moved in a circle around the area where the van had been, but then trotted straight toward the partial boot print. The K-9 sat and stared up at her with his dark brown eyes, as if willing her to understand these two things belonged together.

"Good boy, Ozzy. Good boy!" She took the rope toy from her pocket and tossed it away from the crime scene. Ozzy took off after it like a wolf tracking a rabbit.

"Ashley? What's going on?"

She turned in time to see both Elk Valley Chief of Police, Nora Quan and her task force boss, Chase Rawlston, heading toward her. Behind them, she noted one of her task force teammates, Detective Bennett Ford, speaking with Cade McNeal, while the other task force members hovered nearby, too. Interesting that they'd all come in response to her call. Probably assuming she couldn't handle the kidnapping on her own.

She and Chase lived in Elk Valley, but the rest of the members were from out of state, staying at the local hotel, the Elk Valley Château. They'd flown or driven in for their very first meeting. They were gathering again the following morning, but she had planned to head over to the Château after walking Ozzy in the park, joining them for dinner so they could begin discussing the case.

"Chief. Boss." Ashley nodded at them respectively. "I witnessed a woman being abducted. The same perp, wearing all black with a black ski mask covering his face, tried to grab the baby first, but then took the woman instead. Perp is roughly six feet tall, but rather skinny, not muscular. The vehicle is a possible black Chevy minivan, license plates covered in mud."

"Okay." The chief made a quick call to dispatch, instructing all officers on duty to search for the van. Ashley hoped they'd find it.

"What's in the bag?" Chase gestured to the evidence bag. His K-9, a golden retriever named Dash, sat beside him.

Ozzy returned to her side, leaning forward to sniff Dash, but was well trained enough to stay put.

"A glove from the same person who left this partial print." She gestured to the heel print. "It's larger than my boot, so I believe it's from a man, not a woman. The kidnapped victim was shorter than me by about three inches." She looked closer at the glove in the bag. "This is a man's glove, and it was found close to where the van had been. It's possible our perp dropped it. And if you notice how the heel print is deeper along the back ridge? I think he dug his heel into the snow while tossing the woman in the van and jumping in after her. With Ozzy connecting the glove and heel print, I'm thinking this could be our guy."

Chase raised a brow, his expression seeming to be reluctantly impressed with her assessment. "Good work."

She turned back to look at Cade, still holding the baby. "Cade McNeal is a few years older than the Rocky Mountain Killer victims, but do you think it's at all possible this is connected in some way with that case?"

Chase shrugged. "Not the same MO, none of the other victims had family members abducted. But since Cade McNeal is a rancher, it's an angle we need to eliminate to be sure."

She nodded. "Okay. I can interview him in more depth once Ozzy is finished here. I need to get something belonging to the victim from McNeal, too, so I can have Ozzy search where she's been."

"Good idea." Chase glanced at Nora, who nodded.

"I'll have the crime scene techs scour the area," Nora said. "Maybe we'll find another boot print." The police chief met Ashley's gaze. "You're a witness, so I'd like you to stay involved with this."

"I agree, being a witness and having Ozzy's specialty in tracking makes this a perfect case for you, Ashley." She stared at Chase, hoping he didn't mean what she thought he did. He didn't avoid her gaze, but gestured behind him. "Let's go back and talk to the rest of the team."

"Come, Ozzy." She put the Lab on leash, since the other team members had their K-9s with them. All the dogs were well trained, but they were still dogs and liked to sniff each other. As she hurried to catch up to Chase, she asked, "You're seriously kicking me off the task force?"

"I didn't say that." He shot a narrow glance at her, which she took as a silent warning not to go running to her father to complain, something she'd never do. "We'll keep you updated as part of the team, and I want you to attend the full debrief tomorrow, but this case needs your expertise. A kidnapped woman and a possible infant abduction are high priority. You and Ozzy are already involved and have done good work."

She gritted her teeth to prevent from snapping back at him. He was only saying nice stuff about the job she'd done to soften the blow of being sidelined from the serial murder case.

"Look, I need to get Danny home," Cade was saying as they joined the others. The baby was crying now, and the rancher was swaying from one foot to the other to soothe him. "I need to give him a bottle."

Ashley stood near the tall, muscular, handsome rancher with dark hair and brilliant green eyes. She recognized his name, but he was eight years older than she was, so they never moved in the same social circles.

"Okay, everyone, listen up." Chase took charge and addressed the group. "Ashley has stumbled upon a kidnapping. We're going to keep her in the loop on the task force intel, including the meeting tomorrow, but she's going to work this case until it's solved."

Detective Bennett Ford and sheriff's deputy Selena

Smith exchanged a knowing glance. Bennett's K-9, an adorable beagle named Spike, and Selena's, a male Malinois named Scout, sat calmly next to them. US marshal Meadow Ames and her vizsla, Grace, stood off to the side with Officer Rocco Manelli and his chocolate Lab, Cocoa. Highway patrol officer Hannah Scott gave Ashley a sympathetic look as she rested her hand on her Newfoundland, Captain. And, finally, FBI agent Kyle West and his coonhound named Rocky, stared at her intently. It was the same silent warning Chase had given her.

Ashley felt her cheeks flush as she realized they all had jumped to a similar conclusion. She was being sidelined, because she was a rookie and had only been included on the task force because of her father.

She lifted her chin, determined not to let them see how upset she was. She'd remain professional, no matter what. The task force began to break up to head back to the Château when a pair of headlights cut through the night, catching her attention.

The vehicle moved slowly down the road. Ozzy growled, which caused a few of the other K-9s to shift and look around curiously.

"Easy boy," she said in a low tone as she watched the headlights grow brighter. Without warning, the lights abruptly went dark.

"Did you see that?" Ashley glanced at Chase, who nodded. "I'm taking Ozzy to check it out."

Without waiting for permission, she broke away from the group and ran across the parking lot to the road. Had the assailant in the van come back to find Cade and the baby?

Or was this some other potential crime in progress?

Either way, she couldn't ignore her suspicions. As she reached the road and continued toward the location where she'd seen the headlights, they abruptly snapped back on, blinding her with their intensity.

Then the vehicle surged toward her as the driver had hit the gas.

"Ozzy!" She jumped to the side of the road, tugging her K-9's leash to get him out of the way. The vehicle zoomed past, picking up even more speed as it disappeared around a curve in the road.

"Ashley! Are you okay?" Chase had run over to her, his gaze full of concern. While he might not want her on the team, he probably didn't want to explain to her father she'd been hit by a car, either.

"Did you see it?" She gasped for breath. "Was it a black minivan?"

"It was hard to tell, the driver had his high-beam lights on." Chase stared at the now-empty road. "That guy tried to hit you on purpose."

You think? She bit back the sarcastic reply, her gaze searching and finding rancher Cade McNeal and his infant nephew. "I'd better escort Cade and Danny home." She nodded in their direction. "I have a bad feeling the assailant is going to try again."

"Good idea." Chase lightly clapped her on the back, the most friendly gesture he'd given since the task force had been created. "Be careful. It appears this guy doesn't care who gets in his way."

She nodded and bent to run her hand over Ozzy's soft fur. Oz licked her cheek, as if reassuring her he was okay. Rising to her feet, she walked back toward Cade.

Maybe she wouldn't be actively working with the task force over the next few days, but she made a silent promise to do everything in her power to find this kidnapper and toss him behind bars.

Where he belonged.

TWO

"Mr. McNeal? I'd like to follow you home."

Cade's patience was stretched to the breaking point, his heart tight with Danny's crying and his sister's kidnapping, so he didn't argue. He needed to feed the baby then would gladly help this K-9 cop and her partner find Melissa. "Cade. I'm in that Ram truck."

"I'm in the navy blue SUV with the K-9 logo. I'll be right behind you, okay?"

Giving a curt nod, he grabbed the stroller and strode quickly to his ranch vehicle. He pulled the car seat from the stroller, and fastened Danny inside the rear seat, facing backward, before storing the rest of the stroller on the floor. The process of taking the thing apart and putting it back together again, went smoothly now that he'd mastered the mechanics.

The boy was wailing even more loudly now, making him feel like the worst uncle ever. He should have been better prepared by having another bottle ready to go. Not that he'd anticipated Melissa being kidnapped.

Kidnapped! Who? And why? It didn't make any sense.

They needed to find his sister before something bad happened to her. He pressed the speed limit, urging the truck to eat up the miles. Thankfully, traffic wasn't a huge problem, and he made it to his ranch within fifteen minutes.

"It's okay, Danny. I'll get you a bottle. Hang on, big guy."

He found himself speaking to the baby as if the one-month-old could understand. It made him feel better, anyway. He noticed the dark SUV pull in behind him, but didn't wait. Carrying the infant car seat into the house, he set Danny in the center of the kitchen table and expertly made a bottle.

It didn't take long, which was a good thing because the baby's crying wreaked havoc on his nerves. He deftly unstrapped his nephew from his seat, stripped off his winter coat and hat, then held him in the crook of his arm. He gave the bottle to Danny, and the baby instantly calmed down. Danny's red-rimmed damp eyes seemed to stare up at him reproachfully, silently asking what had taken him so long.

"I'm sorry, buddy." He sighed and pressed a kiss to the baby's forehead. Then he sank into the closest kitchen chair as the pretty, blonde K-9 officer and her black Lab entered the ranch house. He wasn't annoyed since he didn't usually lock the doors.

Although he would tonight. And every night thereafter until Melissa had been found.

"Nice place." She glanced around admiringly. "You and Melissa live here alone?"

"With Danny, yes." He felt calmer now that the baby was cared for. Although the desperate need to find his sister remained. "We inherited the ranch when our parents died in a small plane crash six years ago." He didn't add that he'd been hanging on to the ranch by a wing and a prayer ever since. He'd helped his dad for years, but now he was on his own. Melissa had taken to helping in the kitchen and cleaning, which had been nice.

Now she was gone. He hated that he'd let some masked man grab her. He'd let his sister down, in the worst way possible.

"I'm sorry you've had to go through this, Cade, but I need to ask you a few questions." She glanced at her Lab.

"I also need to feed Ozzy. If you don't mind, I'll bring his food and dishes in."

"Go ahead, Officer Hanson. Make yourself at home." Normally, he didn't like strangers invading his personal space. But nothing about the past hour and a half had been normal.

"Thanks. And please, call me Ashley." She disappeared with her dog, returning a few minutes later. It seemed oddly personal to be together in the kitchen, feeding Danny while she took care of her partner.

"There you go, Ozzy. Such a good boy. Yes, you're a good boy." She smoothed a hand over the dog's ears, then stepped back, giving him a hand signal that must have meant he could eat.

Cade tore his gaze away with an effort. Why was he so fascinated by the pair? Time to get a grip. He'd tried the relationship path. It hadn't gone well. Elaine Jurgen had wanted to be a rancher's wife, without the part where the rancher worked from dawn to dusk and often later. To make matters worse, Elaine had not been at all happy when he'd encouraged Melissa to continue living with him to raise her child at the ranch. Elaine had demanded to know if the two would be living there after their wedding, and he'd confirmed that Melissa and her baby would stay as long as she wanted and needed to. That had sent Elaine into a fit of rage. She'd thrown her engagement ring at him and stormed off.

Months later, she'd called to see how he was doing. The way she'd seemed so concerned and caring toward him had taken him aback after the angry state she'd left him. Their brief conversation had made Cade wonder if her dramatic exit had been carefully orchestrated, and that he was supposed to have followed her out, begging for her to reconsider.

Yeah, he hadn't.

To be honest, he hadn't missed Elaine as much as he'd thought he would. Things had been great at first, but, over time, she'd changed. Or maybe he had. Once she was gone, he'd been relieved not to deal with her incessant complaining. When she'd called, hinting at getting back together, he'd bluntly reminded her that nothing had changed and it was best for her to move on.

She'd ended the call without another word.

As he watched Officer—Ashley care for her K-9 partner, he was annoyed at the spark of interest. *Not happening*, he told himself sternly. Getting tangled in another relationship was out of the question. He didn't have the time or the energy to spare.

Especially with a too young, too pretty, cop. Ashley might be good at her job, but she would have no idea what ranch life was really like. Better for him to stay far, far away.

The subject of his thoughts dropped into the chair next to him. "Your nephew is adorable. How old is Danny?"

"Just over a month." He met her gaze, struck by her clear blue eyes, the color of wildflowers in spring. "I saw the near-miss with that vehicle aiming at you and your dog. I'm glad you're both okay."

"Ozzy, yes." She frowned. "That was too close for comfort. I believe that the kidnapper intended to return to the scene to make another attempt at Danny."

"That possibility occurred to me, too." He sighed, the weight of Melissa's abduction resting heavily on his shoulders. "We need to find my sister. Danny obviously needs his mother. What can I do? What do you need from me?"

She shrugged out of her coat, removed a small notebook from the pocket then sat down. "You mentioned Melissa's ex-boyfriend, a guy named Vincent Orr. We'll check out his current whereabouts, but what about other guys she's been dating?"

He frowned. "I don't know of any, she only had Danny a month ago."

"I understand, but what about her friends? Former co-workers? Someone who might know more about Melissa's personal life."

"Her closest friend is Jessie Baldwin." He was glad to have at least one name to give her. He didn't like feeling inadequate. "Melissa used to work at the Rusty Spoke, it's a cowboy bar and restaurant in town. Jessie worked there, too, and should be able to give you a list of other employees. If there was another guy who'd captured Melissa's interest, she'd know."

"Great, that's a huge help." She scribbled *Jessie Baldwin* on her notepad. "Anyone else?"

He shook his head, feeling his face flush with embarrassment that he wasn't more in tune to his sister's life. Melissa wasn't a kid anymore; he didn't keep track of her comings and goings like an overprotective parent.

Then again, maybe that was the reason Melissa had ended up with a loser like Vincent. And as a single mother.

"Hey, I understand." Ashley smiled sympathetically. "I'm sure running a place like this keeps you busy."

"It does." Speaking of which, he'd need to head out to the barn soon. Glancing down, he noticed Danny had fallen asleep. He set the bottle aside and lifted the boy so that he was up against his shoulder in case he needed to burp.

"Ozzy's expertise is tracking." The dog had finished eating and had come to sit beside her. "I'd like to have something of Melissa's to use as a scent article. Dirty socks work well or a recently worn shirt would be good, too. I plan to have Ozzy do some tracking around the area of the park."

"Dirty socks or a dirty shirt." He raised a brow then

shrugged and nodded. "I'm sure we'll find something in the laundry basket in her room."

"Great." Ashley stroked Ozzy's fur. The dog licked her hand before stretching out on the floor at her feet. Cade had grown up with ranch dogs, mostly border collies trained to herd cattle. Their dog, Skippy, had gone over the rainbow bridge last year and, with Melissa expecting a baby, he had thought it best to wait to get another.

Ozzy was an extremely well-trained dog. Seeing the bond between Ashley and the black Lab made him long for another four-legged friend. Maybe once this nightmare was over, he'd search for another collie.

"Ah, is there something I can do to help?" Ashley glanced around the kitchen. "I know a little about babies from my old babysitting days, and if there's something else you need before I get Melissa's clothing, I'm happy to pitch in."

What he needed was a babysitter so he could get the evening chores done. Thankfully, Melissa had downloaded a baby monitor app to both their phones.

He'd called her cell phone several times while Ashley had been working with Ozzy at the scene, but his calls had gone straight to voice mail.

His stomach churned as he'd realized the kidnapper had probably ditched her phone, cutting off her ability to call him for help. He tried not to think the worst about what the kidnapper's plan for his sister entailed. He silently prayed she wouldn't be harmed. In the meantime, he didn't dare leave Danny alone while he went out to the barn, even with a baby monitor. He swallowed a sigh and stood. "There's a Crock-Pot here with beef stew for dinner. Melissa put it on this morning. Why don't you join me in getting a bite to eat before you and Ozzy go to work? I need to finish taking care of the animals in the barn, too."

She gave him an appraising look. "Okay, that works. We'll eat and I'll watch Danny while you do the evening chores. Then Ozzy and I will head out."

He hesitated. "I appreciate your help, Ashley, but is it wise for you and Ozzy to track Melissa at night? Wouldn't it be better to wait until morning?"

"It's not that late, and I'd rather go now while the trail is fresh." She patted the black Lab's head then rose to join him at the kitchen counter. "The beef stew smells good. We'll eat then get to work. The sooner you finish those chores, the sooner I can get Ozzy on your sister's scent."

He nodded, reaching up to pull two bowls from the cupboard.

His sister needed to be found, and watching the K-9 work the crime scene had impressed him. Yet he wasn't thrilled with the idea of Ashley and Ozzy returning to the park in the darkness.

Reminding himself that Ashley was an armed police officer didn't help. What if this guy returned and managed to kidnap Ashley, too? Ozzy was a tracker, not a guard dog like a German shepherd.

He decided it would be better if they stayed close. He had a hunting rifle, had bagged a deer last fall during the season. He could hit what he was aiming at from at least a couple hundred yards.

Yep. Ashley wouldn't like it, but she wasn't going back to the crime scene alone. Not at night.

Not until this creep was caught.

Ashley was far too aware of Cade McNeal and his cute nephew. He was so sweetly attentive to the child, making her think about one day having a family of her own.

But not now. And, really, she wasn't sure she'd ever settle down. Her parents' marriage had not been the greatest example. Her father had never been home, and his workaholic tendencies had strained their marriage to the breaking point.

Her dad's meddling in her career was his way of trying to make up for lost time. And look how that turned out. She'd already been sidelined from the task force.

Not for long, though. She would go to the meeting tomorrow and insist on being kept in the loop. And once she'd found Cade's missing sister, she'd be back at it.

The baby slept in his seat as they ate the tasty beef stew. Ashley had been surprised at how Cade had offered a heartfelt prayer before the meal.

She had attended church when she was young, but once her parents had begun spending more time apart, that practice had dwindled off and stopped altogether. She was touched at how Cade had prayed for Melissa's safety and for God to guide them to the person responsible.

The minute Cade finished eating though, he jumped to his feet. "I'm sure Danny will sleep for a while yet. I appreciate you staying here while I finish the chores."

"Not a problem." She smiled reassuringly, although eyed the sleeping baby warily. If he woke up, she'd have to take care of him. Hopefully, he wouldn't.

Settling his Stetson on his head, Cade shrugged into the rawhide coat and left. Since Danny was sleeping, she poked around until she found Melissa's bedroom.

There were plenty of dirty clothes in the hamper. Using an evidence bag, she removed a pair of discarded socks and then pulled the edges of the bag together so the socks were inside. Ozzy followed her into the room, sniffing with interest.

There was no doubt in her mind that Ozzy would track Melissa's scent. The way he looked up at Ashley made her think he was ready to get back to work.

"Soon, boy." She patted his head on her way down the hall to the kitchen. "We'll head out soon."

She cleaned the kitchen, putting the leftover stew in a container and then washing and drying the dishes. There was a dishwasher, but the task gave her something to do. She had no idea how long it would take for Cade to care for the animals.

Seeing a computer in the dining room, she crossed over to check it out. Unfortunately, the device was password protected.

Five minutes later, Cade returned. "Did Danny wake up?"

"No. I think all that crying wore him out." She grabbed her coat from the chair. "I'll be back soon."

"Hold on, we're coming with you."

What? She frowned. "No, you're not."

"Yeah, we are." He was putting Danny back in his snowsuit, taking care not to wake him. "I'll stay in the car, but I want to be close at hand if that ski mask guy returns. I'll bring my hunting rifle with me."

"That's very sweet, Cade, but I insist you and Danny stay here." She knew being a female cop was difficult for some people to accept. "Ozzy and I can handle it."

"We're coming." The baby didn't stir as he zipped the snowsuit. "Danny and I can ride along with you and Ozzy, or I'll follow you. Doesn't matter which."

She sighed, searching his gaze. Maybe he was worried about the baby and didn't want to be there alone. That idea made her think having him tag along with her was better in the long run. As she didn't want anything to happen to them, she relented. "Fine. Have it your way. We'll use my SUV because it's set up for Ozzy."

"Thank you." His quiet gratitude eased her annoyance. She understood his concern. Some guy had grabbed Melissa from the park, but how long would it take for the perp to find the address for the ranch?

Not long.

She bent to fasten Ozzy's K-9 vest in place. Then made sure she had the bag with Melissa's socks before heading for the door. Cade was right behind her, carrying Danny's infant seat. He paused to grab a rifle from the locked cabinet, carefully setting it along the floor of the back seat.

To any stranger passing by, they probably looked like a family heading out to shop or have dinner. She gave herself a mental shake as she placed her partner in the back of the SUV. Ozzy didn't mind. When Cade transferred the base of the baby's car seat from his truck to her vehicle, Ozzy pressed his nose up against the grate to sniff Danny.

"How long do you think he'll sleep?" she asked once they were settled in the front.

"No clue. I have a feeling my taking him out for the day has messed up his sleeping schedule." He grimaced. "I hope he's not up all night."

His comment reminded her of a question she'd failed to ask earlier. "Why did you have the baby? And where was Melissa before she showed up at the park?"

"She asked me to take Danny to town when I picked up our supplies. Claimed she hadn't gotten much sleep the night before, so I agreed. I thought it would be good for her to have a nap."

Interesting. "Go on."

"I lingered in town, picking up other items for Danny, too. Melissa texted me that I should meet her at Elk Valley Park at five o'clock in the evening." He raked his hand over his face. "To be honest, I was angry. I'd given her time alone and she'd used it to run off and meet with someone. Why else would she want to meet in town? Next thing I know, some guy in a ski mask is chasing me and Danny, then he grabs Melissa while I do absolutely nothing to stop him."

Ashley glanced at him. "First of all, none of this is your fault, Cade. You had to protect Danny. It's what anyone in your shoes would have done. Second, I am the one who should have questioned you about this sooner. You don't have any idea who she went out to meet?"

"None. If I did, I would tell you."

"I know you would." Her thoughts raced. "Is it possible the masked man snatched her phone? Sent you the text as if it came from her?"

He straightened in his seat. "Yes, absolutely. I should have thought of that. At the time, I didn't understand why on earth she'd ask me to meet at the park."

"There's no way to know for sure if that's the case, I'm just running various scenarios in my head. Hopefully, once Ozzy starts tracking her scent, we'll learn more."

"I pray you will." He fell silent for a moment then said, "I've always leaned on my faith in difficult times. But right now? I'm having trouble staying positive."

Ashley wasn't sure how to respond to that. "I was raised to attend church, but haven't been in years. When you prayed at dinner tonight, it made me want to go back. To see what I've been missing."

His stern features softened into a rueful smile. "I'm glad to hear that. God never promises our lives will be easy. He just wants us to trust in Him. Time for me to do that with this situation, as well."

She nodded, pulled into the parking lot and positioned her SUV so that the headlights were trained on the area where several crime scene markers were still positioned at key locations.

"Stay here." She gave him a narrow look. "I mean it, Cade. I need Ozzy to stay focused."

"I promise."

Somehow, she didn't quite believe him. She handed him the key fob in case he needed to get Danny out of there. Then she pulled out her phone. "I need your number."

He rattled it off and she quickly added him as a contact. Then she called him, so he could do the same. When that was finished, she slid out of the SUV and released Ozzy. She wouldn't put him on leash, but clipped it to her belt in case they stumbled across a wild animal.

"Oz, this is Melissa." She opened the bag for him. He sniffed the dirty socks then lifted his dark eyes to hers. "Seek! Seek Melissa!"

Oz went to work, eager to please. He liked the search-and-find game and was good at it, too.

He picked up Melissa's scent near the spot she'd been abducted. Ashley praised him, but didn't reward him. They weren't done yet.

"Seek! Seek Melissa."

He zigzagged around the parking lot then headed straight for the woods. She turned on her flashlight and followed.

Ozzy took her deep into the woods lining the north side of the park. It wasn't easy to keep on eye on him, since he blended with the night. The white K-9 letters on his vest were the best way to see him. He abruptly stopped nosing the ground near the base of a large oak tree, then sat and looked at her.

Playing the flashlight along the ground, she spied what had gotten his attention. There were several prints in the snow, overlapping, so that she couldn't identify the make and model of the shoe.

"Good boy, Ozzy! Good boy!" She rubbed his silky coat then gave the command. "Seek! Seek Melissa!"

He jumped up and returned to the task of tracking Melissa's scent. He didn't get very far, though, when he alerted again.

Examining the ground, Ashley didn't see anything at first. Then the flashlight beam landed on a rope. The length of twine was about three feet long.

Ozzy sat beside the rope and stared up at her. His dark eyes clung to hers. She understood the binds had been used to hold Melissa.

She rocked back on her heels as the implication sank deep. Someone had tied Melissa here, used her phone to get Cade and Danny to the park, then left her. Only, Melissa had managed to escape, following the assailant in time to shout a warning.

"Good boy!" She pulled Ozzy's favorite rope toy from her pocket and tossed it for him. Even in the darkness, he easily caught it.

This was a good find, and one she needed to call in. Unfortunately, she was no closer to figuring out who'd kidnapped Melissa.

Or why.

THREE

It wasn't easy to sit patiently for Ashley and Ozzy to return. He silently prayed that the K-9 duo would find something useful.

Knowing the kidnapper had likely intended to grab Danny, based on Melissa's crying out for him to keep the baby safe, made him hope that she was still alive and relatively unhurt. It was possible this guy wanted mother and son together for some reason.

To use as leverage over Vincent? A chill snaked down his spine at the possibility. He'd never liked Vincent, and it would not surprise him to discover her ex-boyfriend was involved in something illegal. Especially since it didn't make sense to him that Vincent would resort to kidnapping Melissa and Danny. What would be the end goal? As Danny's father, easily proven by DNA testing, he had rights. Although if Vincent did come back, he'd have to pay child support. Cade had assumed avoiding payments while working for cash was the main reason Vincent had skipped town.

No, there was something more sinister behind all of this. He tried to remember everything Melissa had said about the guy. It made him feel bad to realize he hadn't always paid much attention to her comments. Not because he wasn't interested, but because running the ranch had taken all his time and energy. Turning in his seat, he looked back at Danny. He needed to remember, for the baby's sake.

Hadn't Vincent fixed Melissa's car at one point? Yes, he remembered now. Vincent had been a car mechanic, living over the garage of a service station. Melissa had mentioned Vincent had claimed that by leaving Elk Valley, he could easily find a much better paying job because his skills were in such high demand.

Now, he couldn't help but wonder if Vincent had left for another reason. The money, sure. But why? It wasn't a stretch to think the guy may have owed someone money, either related to drugs or gambling, and had taken off to avoid repaying the debt or to make more money to pay it off.

Cade made a mental note to provide that information to Ashley as soon as possible. Movement across the parking lot had him straightening in the seat. Then he relaxed when he saw Ashley and Ozzy walking toward him. His heart sank when he realized she was on the phone.

Had she found something? His gut knotted with tension, his mind going to the worst-case scenario. *Please, Lord Jesus, not Melissa's dead body. Please?*

Ashley disconnected from the line and approached the SUV. She'd left the motor running to provide warmth for Danny, so he lowered the window. "What did you find?"

"Evidence. My boss is sending the crime scene tech back out here, so this will take a while. Is Danny okay?"

"He's fine, still sleeping. What kind of evidence?" He imagined Ozzy finding a pool of blood in the woods.

She paused then said, "Oz followed Melissa's scent to some footprints and a length of twine. We'll need to test the rope for DNA to prove it was used on Melissa."

He nodded slowly, his thoughts whirling. Twine was better than blood, especially if she'd gotten herself free in time to warn him to protect Danny. It was the only theory that made sense, although he supposed there could be other possibilities. He was a rancher, not a cop.

"How long will it take to get DNA?" He watched Ashley's expression and caught the grimace.

"I'm going to see if the lab will make it a priority, considering your sister is missing and in danger." It wasn't an answer, but he understood it was the best she could do.

"Ozzy's nose really came through for us." He dropped his glance to the dog. The black Lab was a beauty and looked oddly satisfied with his work as his tongue lolled to the side.

"He's amazing." Ashley's smiled down at the K-9. "Once the crime scene tech gets here, we should be able to leave. Oz alerted twice almost right away. I had him searching for a while longer, to make sure there wasn't something we missed. He didn't alert anywhere else so I have to assume Melissa was taken into the woods and came back out along the same path."

"Okay." He was glad Ashley had insisted on coming out tonight. "I thought of something, too."

"Really? What?"

He filled her in on what he remembered of Vincent. It wasn't much, but when he mentioned how Vincent boasted about being able to obtain a higher paying job, and the possibility of someone grabbing Melissa and Danny to get money back from Vincent, she nodded thoughtfully.

"That's one angle to consider." Her eyes brightened with excitement. "We need to follow up on all leads, no matter how slim. We'll dig into Vincent's financial records, see if we can figure out if he was up to something."

For the first time since Melissa had been tossed in the van, he felt useful. "I'm sure someone else has moved into his apartment over the service station, housing isn't easy to find here, but it may not hurt to check it out."

"I'll have an officer go by to make sure Melissa isn't being held there. Although I agree, I'm sure someone has

rented the place by now." Her gaze cut over to where a vehicle was pulling into the parking lot. "Hang tight. I'll be
back soon."

With a nod, he rolled up the window. Thankfully, Danny
was still sleeping, but he remained concerned the baby
would be up at night. Should he wake him? Play with him?
Or just let him sleep?

Melissa was the one who'd gotten up to feed and care
for him. Even though his room wasn't far from hers, he'd
often slept through Danny's crying, physically exhausted
by the seemingly endless list of ranch chores.

Looking at the baby now, he wished he'd paid more attention. "I guess we'll figure it out together, huh, big guy?"

Danny didn't answer.

Cade watched as Ashley and Ozzy led another person,
presumably the crime scene tech, toward the woods. He
could see a pair of flashlights bobbing in the darkness.

A rope and no blood. Oddly, he found that reassuring.
He felt a renewed confidence that Ashley and Ozzy would
find Melissa. They'd already discovered several clues.

Less than fifteen minutes later, Ashley and Ozzy returned. She opened the back so Ozzy could jump inside,
then came around to slide in behind the wheel. "I'm going
to swing by the service garage for a few minutes. Erin, the
crime scene tech isn't sure anyone is living there. Officer
Ed Gerund will meet us there."

"Let's go." The hour was just a quarter past eight, and
the animals expected to be fed early the following morning, but he didn't care. Not if there was even the remot-
est possibility Melissa was being held above that garage.

Besides, they were already in town. May as well check
it out.

"Did you have to get a search warrant?" he asked as
Ashley drove through Elk Valley to the other end of town.

"No, this is exigent circumstances. The missing woman's boyfriend's last residence." She peered through the windshield. "I think it's off Tenth Street."

He worked on his truck himself, so he couldn't say for sure. As they turned down the street, he saw the service station up ahead on the left. "That's it."

"I see it." Ashley frowned. "It looks dark."

"Maybe the owner is still looking for a replacement mechanic? The added perk of living space would be a draw to someone starting out."

"Could be." Ashley pulled into the driveway. "Oz and I will check it out with Gerund. You know the drill, Cade. This is a potentially dangerous situation, especially if the kidnapper is hiding out here. I need you to get behind the wheel and to drive Danny to safety if anything goes wrong."

"Understood." He slid of out the passenger seat and went around to take the wheel. He stood for a moment in the cold night air, watching as Ashley freed Ozzy from the back hatch.

A squad car pulled in behind them and an older officer emerged from behind the wheel.

Ashley acknowledged him with a wave then held the bag for the Lab to sniff. "Melissa. Seek Melissa."

The K-9 wagged his tail and began scouting the area.

Cade's gut clenched when Ashley pulled her weapon. Just a precaution. Right?

Raking his eyes over the building, he didn't see any sign someone was there. As he slid behind the wheel, he whispered a little prayer as Ashley followed Ozzy up the set of stairs to the dark apartment, Officer Gerund behind her. It made sense that the dog would find Melissa's scent, his sister had obviously been here with Vincent at least ten months ago. And if no one else was living there, her scent would have lingered.

He gripped the steering wheel tightly, watching as Ashley rapped on the door then kicked it open. Officer Gerund patted her shoulder, as if saying nicely done. Ozzy followed her inside. Tracking the beam of her flashlight through the windows, Cade waited as she and Gerund searched the place.

When she emerged a few minutes later, Ashley shook her head before returning to street level. While he hadn't really expected her to find Melissa up there, disappointment stabbed deep.

Ashley and Gerund spoke briefly before Ashley walked to the SUV. It was her official police car, so he slid out from behind the wheel. She offered a sweet smile. "Thanks. We're finished here. Ozzy found Melissa's scent, but oddly didn't find any trace of the man who dropped the glove." She frowned, shrugged and then added, "We can head back to the ranch."

"Okay." He went around to get into the passenger seat. "Does this mean that Vincent isn't the kidnapper?"

She pursed her lips. "Maybe. I hate to jump to conclusions, but I expected Ozzy to alert. Vincent could easily be working with someone else. Or someone is out to get him. There are various scenarios that might explain the fact Ozzy didn't alert on Glove Guy's scent."

"Yeah." Ashley was right to be cautious. Yet he kept wondering if Vincent had left town for a darker reason than just not wanting to be a father to Danny. Or to pay child support, for that matter.

As they drove back to the McNeal Four, he glanced at Ashley. "You'll keep me updated on your progress?"

"Absolutely." She hesitated before adding, "I don't want you to take this the wrong way, Cade. But I think it's best if Ozzy and I stay at the ranch tonight. I'll sleep on the sofa, just in case this guy comes back."

He was hit with dueling emotions. Having her stay at the ranch would be a pain, infringing on his privacy. Yet he also liked the idea of having her and Ozzy close in case the assailant did return.

"Yeah, sure." He didn't see how he could gracefully decline her offer. "You can use the guest room. It will be more comfortable than the sofa."

"Thanks, Cade." She smiled warmly, making the knots in his stomach tighten.

Yeah, somehow he sensed this was not a good idea. At least, for him personally. Looking at Danny's car seat in the rearview mirror, he reminded himself the baby was more important than his turbulent emotions.

Then again, he'd suffer just about anything to protect the little boy from harm.

Anything.

From the tightness of Cade's jaw, Ashley sensed he wasn't thrilled with her plan of spending the night. Too bad. No way was she going to let anyone touch this baby.

Besides, her long day was catching up with her. She was tired and Ozzy needed time to rest, too. Driving back and forth from her place to the ranch would take too much time away from the case. She needed to find Melissa so she could get back to working with the task force. She needed to prove that she was an asset to the team, not a hindrance. That she truly belonged, not just because her father asked for her to be included. Current kidnapping aside, this was her first big case and she didn't want to let the opportunity slip through her fingers.

"I'll stay out of your way," she offered, breaking the silence.

He paused for several heartbeats. "I'm not concerned about you and Ozzy getting in the way. You've already helped me out by watching Danny while I went out to finish my chores."

The unspoken question made her smile. "I'm happy to help keep an eye on Danny in the morning, too. But I can't stay too long, I'll have to head out shortly after breakfast to follow up on other possible leads. And to attend another meeting at the precinct."

"Thanks. I understand. I won't keep you from your job." He shot her a glance. "I appreciate everything you've done so far to locate my sister. I'm convinced you and Ozzy will find her."

She flushed at his kind words, hoping he wouldn't notice in the darkness. "That's my job." She kept her tone light. "And Ozzy's, too. He loves tracking scents."

"He does seem to enjoy the task," Cade agreed. "Honestly, I've never seen anything like it."

"I've been honored and blessed to have been chosen as Ozzy's handler. He's the best partner any cop could ask for."

"It's obvious you make a great team." Cade fell silent, seemingly lost in thought.

She'd been disappointed the apartment above the service garage had been empty. Ozzy had alerted in one room, which she'd believed to be the main bedroom. Once she'd praised and rewarded him for that find, she'd asked him to "Seek glove."

But that search had come up empty.

Even though she'd agreed with Cade that Vincent would have visitation rights and therefore had no reason to kidnap his girlfriend and his son, she had thought he may have met with the bad guy in the apartment at some point. But that hadn't seemed to be the case.

She yawned, raising a hand to cover her mouth. Maybe they'd find something in searching through Vincent Orr's financial records. To do that, they needed a warrant. She'd have to ask Nora about that tomorrow.

Meanwhile, she planned to search Melissa's room in more depth. There could be something in there that would lead them to the abductor.

There had been nothing obvious when she'd gone in to get Melissa's socks. The room had been surprisingly tidy, the top of her dresser cleared, and there hadn't been anything other than a book on the nightstand. But most women wouldn't leave love notes or other personal gifts from a boyfriend out in plain sight. If Melissa had anything, she'd tucked it away.

Ashley left the highway to take the winding road to the ranch. She'd only seen it in the dark, but imagined the view of the Laramie Mountains was stunning during the daytime.

"Do you mind if I look through Melissa's room?" she asked as he indicated she pull the SUV into the spacious three-car garage. "I won't make a mess or anything, but there might be some clue as to who she's been in contact with."

"Fine with me." He turned to face her. "Just let me know if you find something useful."

"I will." She pushed out of the vehicle and went around back to get Oz. She also had a duffel back there, with a small toiletry kit and a change of clothes, both casual civilian clothes and a fresh uniform. She'd wanted to be prepared in the event she'd have to leave Elk Valley at a moment's notice to follow up on a task force lead. Now, she had to hope that Chase would honor his promise of keeping her in the loop on their meetings.

Cade had unbuckled the infant carrier from the back seat, so she and Oz followed him inside. She'd walked Ozzy enough that he shouldn't need to go out yet. After going through Melissa's room, she planned to take the dog around the ranch house, to familiarize herself with the surrounding landscape. There were no streetlights out here, but she had noticed two spotlights mounted on the outside corner of the barn. No doubt, Cade left them on so he could get back and forth in the dark.

Danny began to cry as Cade removed the baby's hat and snowsuit. Of course, now that it was close to bedtime, the baby was awake and wanting attention.

She watched for a moment as Cade lifted the baby in his arms. The way he spoke to the little boy, much the way she talked to Oz, made her smile. The tough rancher was mush when it came to his nephew.

"I need to change him. You'll find the guest room this way." Cade indicated with a tilt of his head that she should follow him down to the bedrooms. "Melissa has been keeping Danny in the room next to hers. I hope Danny's crying doesn't bother you and Ozzy too much."

She noticed the guest room was right across from the nursery. Cade's room was at the end of the short hallway. "Don't worry about it. I appreciate you allowing us to stay."

"No problem." He disappeared into the nursery with Danny.

Ashley set her duffel on the bed, then shrugged out of her coat. The room was nice, although it didn't appear to have been used recently.

Reminding herself that Cade's personal life wasn't any of her business, she crossed the hall to the missing woman's bedroom. It felt wrong to poke around, breaching the young mom's privacy, but it was necessary. The first twenty-four hours were key in any missing person's case.

Picking up the book on the nightstand, she flipped through the pages. A small cocktail napkin fell to the floor.

She bent down to get it, noting it was from the Rusty Spoke bar and restaurant.

Not especially helpful, since Melissa had worked there. Verifying there were no notes on the napkin, she tucked it back inside the book and continued searching. Going through Melissa's clothing in her dresser drawers, she found a small baggie with two hundred dollars in various bill denominations. "Mad money," her mother would have called it. Her mother had saved a wad of cash, aka mad money, before she'd walked out on her father.

But other than the napkin and the cash, she found nothing remotely interesting.

Was the room too clean? She stood for a moment, her hands on her hips as she looked around. Ozzy was stretched out on the floor in the doorway, his dark eyes watching her intently.

"I don't know, Oz, what do you think?" She would have expected to find something indicating Melissa had been seeing someone.

Then again, they didn't have Melissa's phone, either. Over dinner, Cade had mentioned he'd been unable to reach his sister, the calls had gone straight to voice mail. And his attempt to use the Find My Phone app, hadn't worked, either.

Whoever had taken Melissa's phone had turned it off or smashed it to bits.

Another yawn caught her off guard. She gave herself a shake and left Melissa's room. "Come, Ozzy. We need to take a walk outside now."

"Where are you headed?" Cade asked with a frown. He had Danny nestled in the crook of his arm, the baby's eyes were open and looking around curiously. She noticed he'd taken his hunting rifle from the SUV and tucked it in the corner of the living room. She could understand why Cade would want to keep it nearby.

"I want to walk around your house so that we are familiar with the area." She smiled. "We won't be gone long."

He held her gaze for a moment. "If you're not back in ten minutes, I'll head out to look for you."

Was ten minutes enough time? Hopefully. She nodded. "Okay, that's fine. But I'm armed and Ozzy will be on alert, too."

"Be careful." Cade turned and headed to the living room. There, he sat on the sofa and held Danny on his knee. He made funny faces at the baby, making him smile.

Completely adorable. Tearing her eyes from them, she grabbed her jacket. "Come, Ozzy."

The K-9 wagged his tail as he followed her outside.

She took a moment to orient herself, keeping Ozzy off leash for now. Facing the house, the barn was to the left. The lights were positioned so that they illuminated the area between the house and barn. There was a paddock next to the barn, and beyond that what seemed to be a large fenced-in area. Possibly one of the pastures for Cade's cattle.

Rounding the corner, the backside of the house was completely dark. She flipped on her flashlight, holding it with her left hand, resting her right on the butt of her weapon. "Come, Oz."

She walked along the east side of the house. Through the window, she saw Cade sitting on the sofa with the baby. Upon turning the next corner, she envisioned this was where bedrooms were located.

There was a grassy area back here, but thirty yards away, there were thick trees. Hard to tell at night, but she thought there may also be a small hilly section tucked back there.

She used her flashlight to scan the woods. Ozzy began

growling low in his throat. Her partner didn't growl often, so she quickly pulled her weapon.

A second later, the sharp retort of gunfire reverberated through the night.

"Oz!" She instinctively clicked off the flashlight, returned fire, and then dropped to cover the dog with her body.

The kidnapper was out there!

FOUR

Was that gunfire?

Cade leaped off the sofa, his heart thudding in his chest. He took a moment to place Danny in his infant seat, then locked him in the master bedroom. Reaching for his rifle, he opened the side door to go outside.

"Ashley!" He quickly moved along the wall of the house, listening intently.

"Cade! Stay back." Hearing Ashley's voice was reassuring, but he wasn't about to stay back. He peeked around the corner and caught a glimpse of her pale gray slacks in the darkness.

"I'll cover you! On the count of three, ready?" He lifted his rifle toward the sky. "One, two, three!" He fired off two rounds.

Ashley ran toward him, Ozzy a dark shadow at her side. When they were safely around the corner, they wasted no time in heading inside the ranch house.

"Thanks." Ashley's tone came out somewhat grudgingly. As if she didn't like his having to come out to provide cover.

"We're in this together." He blew out a breath then double-checked to make sure all the doors were locked. He set the rifle in the corner, making a mental note to clean the barrel.

"I wish we could head out to track this guy. But it's too dangerous at night. I can't put Ozzy in harm's way." Ashley's grim expression betrayed her frustration. She pulled out her phone. "I'm calling this in."

He nodded and quickly went to the master bedroom to check on Danny. The baby was fine, but he lifted him into his arms and cradled him close anyway. Kissing the boy's head, he inhaled the sweet scent of his baby shampoo.

Cade knew he would do anything to keep this little boy safe. And if that meant shooting an intruder who threatened to harm his nephew, then so be it.

Ashley and Ozzy came to find him a few minutes later. "Is he okay?" A frown furrowed her brow.

"Yes." He met her stare. "What's the plan?"

"I have a couple of officers, including Officer Gerund, who helped me out earlier, coming here. I'm waiting to hear back from my chief about having an officer stationed outside the ranch house tonight."

He tried not to grimace. Not that he resented the extra protection, but he struggled with a bit of guilt over pulling limited resources from the city. Yet what option did he have? The situation was grim. "I can't leave the ranch. There's no one else to take care of the animals."

"I know." Her smile didn't quite reach her beautiful blue eyes. "Hopefully, we'll get approval to have someone stationed outside as a deterrent."

He wasn't so sure one cop would provide that, since this guy had already taken a shot at Ashley and Ozzy. Although it was possible the intent had been to scare them off.

Or provide a diversion so someone else could get close enough to make a grab for Danny.

He didn't like it and wondered again where Melissa was. He desperately needed to believe she hadn't been harmed.

Or worse, killed.

Ashley's phone rang, jarring him from his grim thoughts. As he listened to Ashley's conversation with Chief Nora

Quan, he set Danny back in his infant seat and walked from window to window, making sure they were securely locked and that there was no one lurking outside.

Seeing nothing alarming, he returned to Danny. The baby had fallen asleep again, which was a good thing. He'd read in Melissa's baby books that young infants slept up to eighteen hours a day, even though they also needed to be fed often.

He tucked Danny's car seat on the floor near his bed, away from the window. The bed would shield the baby on the off chance someone tried to shoot through the window.

Then again, if the kidnapper wanted the baby, shooting randomly through a window wasn't likely. Cade tried to understand what the kidnapper's purpose was. A plan to use Melissa and Danny as leverage over Vincent only worked if the guy actually cared about them. Something he found difficult to believe.

"Cade?" Ashley's voice came from the doorway. He moved toward her, so they wouldn't disturb the baby.

"What is it?"

"Officer Ed Gerund is going to stay in his squad outside for the next four hours. Another officer will take over after that." Ashley gave a slight shrug. "I'd feel better having more than one cop outside, but this is the best I can do. Chief Quan also asked me to stay close to you while working the case."

"That's good news. Thanks." He glanced over his shoulder at the sleeping baby then gestured to Ashley to back up. He headed for the kitchen. "I want to make sure I have a bottle ready to go for the next time Danny wakes up."

"Good idea." Ashley reached down to stroke Ozzy's black pelt.

He couldn't make the formula completely without refrigerating it. But he added the powder to the bottle and left it on the counter, ready to go. When that was finished, he turned to face her. "Do you need anything else?"

"No, we're good." She searched his face for a moment. "We'll keep you and Danny safe."

"I know." He didn't doubt her dedication one bit, yet he could also take care of himself. "Promise me you'll protect Danny first, okay?"

She hesitated, as if she wanted to protest, then slowly nodded. "Yes. I promise."

"Good." Feeling reassured, he gestured to the bedrooms. "Again, please make yourself at home. Good night, Ashley."

"Good night, Cade." She followed him down the hallway, taking Ozzy with her into the guest room.

He stared at the closed door for a long moment before heading into the master suite. This odd awareness he felt toward Ashley had to stop. He had much bigger issues to worry about, like finding his sister and keeping his nephew safe.

Cade managed to get three hours of sleep before Danny needed to be fed. After that, he was able to get another three hours. At this point, the hour was early enough that there was no use trying to sleep longer. He needed to take care of the animals, then cook breakfast.

One thing about working the ranch, it was physical work. Skipping meals wasn't an option.

To his surprise, Ashley and Ozzy came out to join him fifteen minutes after he'd finished feeding Danny.

She yawned as she shrugged into her winter coat. "I'll be back in a few minutes."

Understanding she needed to take care of her partner, he nodded. While he waited, he broke a half dozen eggs into a bowl and whisked them together.

Ashley and Ozzy returned several minutes later. "The

police officer stationed outside all night reported everything was quiet. Officer Rolland is heading back to town."

"Good news." He set the bowl aside. "If you don't mind, I'd like to take care of the animals before making breakfast. There's plenty of coffee. I fed Danny, so he shouldn't need anything."

"Not a problem." She smiled at the baby. "I don't mind watching him while you finish the morning chores. But I do have a meeting in town at nine sharp."

"Understood." He reached for the rifle, taking it with him in the event someone was out there waiting for him. He'd never had to clear the barn of possible intruders before getting to work, but that's exactly what he did this morning.

Once he was satisfied that he was alone with the livestock, he began feeding and watering the horses. He ignored the pang of concern about Ashley leaving the ranch for her meeting. He and Danny should be safe enough in broad daylight.

He hoped.

Making quick work of the chores, he considered the possibility of asking Roger, the neighboring rancher, to help him out until they found Melissa. It wouldn't be easy for Roger, he was older and had his own work to do. Cade hated to put the rancher out unless it was absolutely necessary. Cade didn't like asking for help, but he also knew he'd readily jump in to assist Roger, as needed.

Had in fact, done that very thing when Roger's wife, Barbara, was sick. She was fine now, but one thing ranchers learned was that they were always stronger together.

When he entered the kitchen an hour later, he was surprised when the scent of hickory-smoked bacon wafted toward him.

"Oh, good. You're back." Ashley glanced at him from the stove. "I'll make the eggs now."

"Ah, you didn't have to do this." He washed his hands at the sink. "I would have made breakfast."

"Easier for me to take care of it." She nodded at the clock. "I told you about my meeting, and I also want to see if Ozzy can pick up the perp's scent outside the property."

"He didn't alert last night, did he?" Cade glanced at the dog, who had stretched out on the floor near the table where Danny was sleeping in his infant seat. Labs were generally good-natured pups, but he sensed Ozzy wouldn't take kindly to anyone trying to hurt the baby.

"No, but we didn't get much beyond the house itself." Using a spatula, she stirred the scrambled eggs. "Have a seat. This is just about finished."

"Thank you." He was touched by her willingness to pitch in and help in a task that was far outside her job description. When he found himself comparing Ashley's easygoing nature to Elaine's, he quickly blocked them.

Ashley was off limits. She was doing her job, and helping him at the same time. Nothing more. Nothing less.

He wasn't interested in getting involved in another messy relationship. No matter how attractive Ashley might be.

End. Of. Story.

"Here you go." Ashley put a plate full of scrambled eggs, bacon and toast in front of him. Then she brought a second plate to the table for herself.

"This looks great." He cleared his throat. "I'd like to say grace."

"I thought you might." She smiled and bowed her head.

It took a moment to gather his thoughts. "Dear Lord, we thank You for this wonderful food. We also thank You for keeping us safe in Your care. Please watch over us, especially Danny, Ashley and Ozzy as we search for Melissa. Amen."

"Amen," Ashley murmured. Lifting her head, she looked

at him. "You should have included yourself, too, Cade. Danny and Melissa need you."

He nodded, but quickly took a bite of his food. He wanted to keep the ranch in the family, especially for Danny, the next generation of the McNeals. Yet it was sobering to acknowledge that Danny and Melissa would be okay without him. Financially, anyway. His sister could sell the ranch and have enough to provide for herself and her son. The thought saddened him, but if that was how this nightmare ended, he'd accept the result. He'd readily give up his life for his sister and her son.

But first, they had to find her.

When breakfast was finished, Ashley took Ozzy outside. Offering the glove to her partner, she commanded him to seek.

Excited to work, Ozzy began sniffing the area, alternating between keeping his nose to the ground and lifting it in the air to catch a scent. Weapon in hand, she kept a keen eye out for danger as they patrolled the property.

They couldn't work for too long; she did not want to be late for the task force meeting. Ozzy didn't alert anywhere near the house or between the path from the house to the barn.

Either the shooter had been someone else or he hadn't come too close. She stood for a moment, scanning the wooded area in front of the low hilly mountains. Truthfully, the shooter could have taken up a position just about anywhere. Most ranchers in the area were good with a rifle, from hunting or protecting their herd from predators.

She would need help to comb the woods, but there wasn't time for that anyway. She told Ozzy to get busy, his cue to go to the bathroom. When she'd cleaned up after him, she headed back inside.

Cade glanced at her while finishing the dishes. "Are you heading to town?"

"Yes. I don't think you should stay here alone, though. It's better for you and Danny to ride with me."

His brows pulled together in a frown. "Do you think that's necessary?"

"I do. Our task force meeting should only take an hour or so. Afterward, I'd like a couple of the team members to return with us so we can search the woods."

Cade glanced at Danny then nodded. "Okay, that's fine. I have work that needs to get done, but nothing that can't wait for a few hours."

"Great." She was relieved he didn't insist on staying behind. "Let's get ready to roll."

"That takes longer than usual these days." He offered a wry smile as he filled a diaper bag with several baby bottles, a pack of diapers and a change of clothes for Danny. Then he bundled the child in his winter coat and hat.

Once they were settled in her SUV, with Ozzy in the back, she glanced at Cade. "I forgot to ask you last night about your involvement in the Young Rancher's Club." Despite that it didn't seem likely the McNeal situation was linked to the Rocky Mountain Killer case, she needed to rule out any connection.

Cade shook his head. "I wasn't involved at all. I'm thirty-four and was a couple years older than the victims. Frankly, I didn't have much interest in joining anyway."

"Why not?" She was curious about his perspective.

"Being in a club like that wasn't my thing." He sent her a sidelong glance. "Seth Jenkins and Brad Kingsley enjoyed the party scene. As I was four or five years older, I was beyond that type of lifestyle. Granted, I wasn't into the party atmosphere when I was younger, either."

She sensed a seriousness about Cade. Interesting that

he'd been that way even before his parents had died. "How well did you know the victims from ten years ago?"

He made an impatient sound. "I just told you, I didn't hang out with them, or consider them friends. Not that I think they deserved to be shot," he hastily added. "I'm sorry I can't help you more. Trevor Gage knows them better than I do. But I think he and his family moved away after the murders."

"Yes, they did move to Salt Lake City, Utah. I think he's some kind of consultant now." She knew Chase had already reached out to Trevor. The guy had an alibi for the timeframe of the murders, so he wasn't considered a suspect. But she'd heard Chase mention Trevor needed to be careful because he may be targeted by the killer. All the guys who'd been members of the YRC ten years ago were possibly in danger.

She was glad to know that group didn't include Cade.

"I can't believe those murders were never solved," Cade said with a frown. "And that the killer is back. When I was getting supplies, many of the locals expressed their concern about where these new murders would lead. No one wants to believe the killer is someone they know."

"I'm sure there is a lot of anxiety over this. Just know there's a whole team of us working to change that." She injected confidence in her tone. She made a mental note to check in with Chase on where things stood with the case, very soon.

"I believe you will," Cade assured her.

Ashley parked in front of the Elk Valley police station at a quarter to nine. "You and Danny can wait for us inside."

He nodded, slinging the diaper bag over his shoulder and heading into the building carrying Danny's car seat. Ashley and Ozzy followed. When she had Cade and Danny settled in the lobby, she took a moment to check in with

Nora, asking about Melissa's phone records. Nora promised Isla would have them soon. Ashley knew their tech analyst would do her best as time was of the essence.

Despite being fifteen minutes early, Ashley frowned when she entered the conference room. She appeared to be the last one to arrive.

Well, except for Chase, their team leader. He walked in a minute after she dropped into a seat beside Highway patrol officer Hannah Scott and her K-9, Captain. Ozzy and Captain touched noses, but stayed beside their handlers. Hannah gave her a warm smile, tucking a strand of her red hair behind her ear. Ashley liked her and appreciated the silent support she'd offered last night.

"Thanks to all of you for arriving so promptly," Chase opened the meeting by saying. The FBI special agent in charge was tall and muscular, with brown hair and intense brown eyes. He gestured to a large whiteboard behind him, where he had already written the names of the three Rocky Mountain Killer victims from ten years ago. Seth Jenkins, Brad Kingsley and Aaron Anderson on one side of the board under a heading of Original Murders in Elk Valley, Wyoming. He'd written the two names of their most recent victims—Henry Mulder, victim #4, in Montana, and Peter Windham, victim #5, in Colorado—on the other side of the board.

It was sobering to realize there was space below Peter's name for additional victims if they discovered any.

Centered between the names Chase had written UNSUB RMK with a question mark after it. Ashley knew from her father that the Feds referred to an unknown subject, in this case their killer, as an unsub.

"Okay, we know the 9mm slugs taken from all five victims are from the same weapon. We also know all the victims have a connection to the Young Rancher's Club."

Chase raked his gaze over the team. "The biggest question facing us is why now? What happened that caused our unsub to begin killing again ten years after the initial three murders?"

"The note our killer left on the victims indicates they got what they deserved, and there are more to come," Bennett Ford said. The detective had short blond hair and light brown eyes, but she noticed he rarely smiled. Next to Chase, he was the most serious member of the group. "Whoever this guy is, he plans to finish what he started."

"Yes, but why the sudden resurgence after ten years?" FBI agent Kyle West asked. "Do we think this guy was in jail and just got out?"

"That's one possibility," Chase admitted. "Isla Jimenez, our tech analyst, has a theory, too. Isla?"

Ashley knew Isla. She worked as a technical analyst for the Elk Valley PD and had been recruited for the task force by Chase himself. The pretty woman with long brown hair and light brown eyes went up to stand beside Chase. She used a marker to add "Semiformal Dance" beneath the word "unsub."

"Our recent victims were killed on Valentine's Day," Isla said. "And going back ten years, the first three victims were also killed on Valentine's Day, or sometime in the early hours of the morning following it. For those of you who may have been here back then, there was a semiformal dance held in the town hall about a month prior to Valentine's Day." She set the marker down. "I think we need to consider something may have happened during or after the dance that caused our killer to take out three members of the Young Rancher's Club."

There was a murmur among the task force members as they digested that connection. Ashley had been only sixteen at the time but she had been at the dance. Chase noticed her reaction.

"Do you remember anything about that night Ashley?" he asked.

"Now that you mention it, I do." She swallowed hard and stood to address the group. "Several of the guys from the Young Rancher's Club, led by our first three victims, Seth, Brad and Aaron, laughed and threw paper spitballs at Naomi Carr when she arrived at the dance. She'd been invited to the dance by Trevor Gage. But the guys jeeringly told her it was a joke, no one wanted her there. They were so mean and callous that Naomi turned and ran out of the town hall, crying. Trevor tried to stick up for her, but the rest of the guys didn't listen." She frowned, reflecting on those chaotic days after the murders. At sixteen, it wasn't easy to consider her friends as potential suspects. "I will say Peter Windham looked upset about it, and quickly followed Naomi outside. If this incident had sparked the series of crimes, it's hard to understand why Peter was killed."

"The prank is a possible connection," Chase mused.

"We need to consider Naomi as a possible suspect." Agent Kyle spoke up. "She has motive for seeking revenge."

"Naomi would never kill anyone." Ashley's protest was a knee-jerk reaction. She swallowed hard, reminding herself not to make snap judgments, but it wasn't easy. "Granted, I was young back then, but I saw Naomi as sweet and kind, much like Peter. We all hung out on occasion, and they never said a bad word about anyone."

"Everyone has secrets." Bennett scowled darkly. "You might think you know someone, then you quickly realize you didn't know them at all."

Ashley eyed him warily. He seemed to be speaking from personal experience. "That's true," she agreed.

"We need to keep an open mind." Chase took control of the discussion. "Isla, check Naomi's background."

Isla nodded and began working her laptop computer.

Chase continued. "We need to reinterview everyone involved, going all the way back to ten years ago. Maybe we'll learn something new, or maybe someone will admit to covering up the truth. We won't know until we turn over every rock and look inside every cranny."

"I see that Naomi Carr-Cavanaugh's parents died five years ago. Her husband died recently, too," Isla said. "She does have an older brother in town, Evan Carr."

"Evan and Naomi weren't close," Ashley felt compelled to point out. "He's much older and didn't hang around with us."

"Noted," Chase said.

"Naomi also doesn't have a gun registered to her name," Isla continued. "Not in her husband's name, either."

"Thanks, Isla. We'll still need to consider her a suspect. And we have a lot of ground to cover." Chase picked up a notepad and began doling out tasks for the team to complete. When he'd finished, Ashley's face burned as she realized she was the only one not given an assignment.

She avoided looking around the room at her colleagues. The last thing she wanted was their pity.

But this was a clear indication that Chase wasn't going to involve her in the task force any more than necessary.

The only thing she could do was to work twice as hard to solve Melissa's kidnapping case. Then he'd have to take her seriously.

At least, she hoped so.

FIVE

Sitting around doing nothing grated on Cade's nerves. He desperately wanted Melissa home, more than anything, and knew that police work took time. He was accustomed to hard labor, long hours, and to feeling productive and accomplished by the end of the day. There were endless ranch chores needing his attention.

Yet he didn't see how he'd get any of them done. Maybe he needed to hire a nanny, someone to keep an eye on the baby so he could get back to work. Yet there was still the danger to contend with, so he'd need someone who could take care of an infant and handle a gun.

A gun-toting nanny? He rubbed his temple. Obviously, he needed more sleep.

The Elk Valley police station was busy with officers coming and going. He and Danny drew attention as they passed by. Struggling to be patient, Cade avoided glancing at the clock. Watching the time wouldn't hurry the meeting along. And, really, he understood the importance of finding the person who'd taken the lives of five men.

Three unsolved murders in Elk Valley and Melissa's kidnapping, plus two murders clearly connected to the cold case. Elk Valley wasn't normally a hot bed of crime. Sure, they had some drug issues and thefts. Disorderly conduct by the cowboys, especially during the rodeo season. But nothing like this.

When the door to the conference room opened, he shot

to his feet. Ashley was one of the first to step through the doorway, followed by the other members of the task force. He hadn't been formally introduced but had interacted with a few on the night of Melissa's kidnapping.

Was that really only fifteen hours ago?

The somber expression on Ashley's face gave him pause, but she managed a tight smile. "Hope you didn't mind waiting."

He shook his head, despite his impatience. It wasn't her fault that he was in this situation. "We're fine. What's the plan?" She'd mentioned something about searching for evidence.

"I'd like to put Ozzy to work for a bit." She paused, glancing over her shoulder at the cadre of task force members. "Excuse me, Meadow? Would you and your K-9 partner Grace have some time to help me search for a sign of the gunman who shot at us last night?"

"Of course." US Marshal Meadow Ames, looked concerned. "Grace's specialty is tracking, just like Ozzy's." The beautiful vizsla wagged her tail at the sound of her name. "I can give you a few hours before I have to drive back to Montana."

"Thanks. This is Cade McNeal, you probably remember him from yesterday. It's his sister who was kidnapped."

"I remember." Meadow gave him a somber nod. "I'm sure this has been difficult."

You have no idea, he thought with a sigh. "Anything you can do to help find this guy would be great."

"Let's do it," Ashley said. "Meadow, you and Grace can follow us back to the McNeal ranch."

"Sounds good. I can hit the road after the search," Meadow said. "Come, Grace."

Soon they were back on the highway. Cade was glad to be heading home, although he didn't think he'd be able to work the ranch while the officers were scouring the woods behind the ranch house. He had an infant carrier backpack that he could use to hold Danny against his chest, but wasn't sure if that was safe enough.

"I hope we can find some trace of the shooter." Ashley frowned. "We don't have a lot to go on."

"What about Melissa's phone records?" He remembered her saying something about getting those. "I tried tracking her phone again earlier, but it's still offline."

Ashley sent a sympathetic glance. "Isla, our tech specialist, is working with the phone carrier to obtain your sister's phone records, and she's asking for a warrant for Vincent's financial records, too. She'll send me the reports when they're available."

Was it his imagination or did it seem like the investigation was taking longer than it should? He swallowed his protest. No point in badgering Ashley. She was doing her best.

But is her best good enough?

He shut down the doubting voice in his head. Ashley and Ozzy had made strides last night. First, finding the glove and boot print, then the binds that had been used to restrain his sister. Not to mention, being nearly run over and shot at.

"As soon as we finish searching the woods, I can watch Danny if you have more chores to do." Her kind offer made him feel even worse about his doubting thoughts.

"Thanks, that would be great." He glanced back at his nephew. "I was thinking I could take Danny with me out to the barn, if you think it's safe enough."

She pursed her lips. "Let's see what we find in the woods first. I don't mind helping, I'd feel better knowing the two of you were safe."

"Okay." He wasn't going to argue.

"I also need to head to the Rusty Spoke to talk to Melissa's coworkers," Ashley continued. "Maybe we can do that after you get a few ranch tasks completed? We can always grab a bite to eat, too."

"Sure." There was no point in telling her the ranch chores were never complete. "Lunch sounds like a great idea." That made him think about dinner, too, and he made a mental note to pull something easy to make out of the freezer. Managing the ranch chores along with the household needs would be difficult.

But not impossible.

Determined to stay positive, to believe that Melissa would soon be found, Cade focused on what needed to be done, prioritizing the list of chores. Yet the moment they arrived back at the ranch, Danny began to cry.

Best laid plans. "It's okay, big guy. I'll get a bottle for you soon."

"I'd offer to help, but Meadow and Grace can't stay too long. They need to head back to Montana." Ashley gestured to the SUV that pulled up alongside them.

"That's fine." Danny was his responsibility.

He watched as Meadow and her K-9, Grace, a tan dog with long, floppy ears followed Ashley and Ozzy along the side of the ranch house. Ashley had the glove in an evidence bag hanging from her utility belt and he knew both K-9s would use it as a scent tracker.

While feeding Danny, he sat on the edge of Melissa's bed, watching the two women working their way through the woods. Meadow had long dark hair and green eyes. She was pretty enough, but his gaze clung to Ashley.

Enough. He gave himself a mental shake. Ashley seemed to care about the ranch chores, and had willingly chipped in to help, but she was a cop. He wasn't interested in a woman who might trample all over his heart. Elaine had changed over time, turning into someone he barely recognized. What if Ashley did that, too? She seemed genuine, but he wasn't sure he could trust his instincts when it came to reading people. Maybe he was just better with animals.

And babies. He glanced down at his nephew's peaceful face. This was all he cared about. Danny and Melissa. The only thing he wanted or needed from Ashley was to find his sister.

And to keep the little boy safe from harm.

Ashley was grateful for Meadow and Grace's help in combing the woods for the shooter. They split the area in two, Ashley and Ozzy taking the section to the right, Meadow and Grace heading to the left.

In Ashley's mind, she believed the shooter had been positioned somewhere on the right. Sounds at night could be deceiving, though, so she hadn't mentioned her thought to Meadow. At the time, she'd been too busy ducking and protecting Ozzy to know for sure.

The terrain was a bit slippery due to the patches of snow and ice. Thankfully, the March wind wasn't as strong today.

"Seek Glove! Seek!" She gave the command while knowing Ozzy didn't need to be talked into playing the search game. He alternated between lifting his head to the air and sweeping the ground as he wound his way between the trees.

When they'd made it through the woods, Ozzy didn't hesitate to take the incline, moving uphill. She gamely followed her partner, trusting him completely.

They were far enough away from Meadow and Grace that she couldn't hear them working the other half of the woods.

She forced Ozzy to stop after twenty minutes for a short break, careful not to overwork the animal. She gave him a sip of water from a collapsible bowl and hugged him to her. He looked up at her with bright eyes, as if asking why they were stopping. After a few minutes, she decided to keep going for another fifteen minutes, tops.

"Seek, Oz. Seek!"

Her K-9 didn't need the command. He put his nose to the ground and scrambled forward several feet. Then he abruptly jutted left, heading to a large leafless tree.

He sat, turning his head to look at her expectantly.

Ashley's heart thudded in her chest as she hurried up the incline to join him. "Good boy, Oz," she praised while scanning the ground.

A glint of metal between two rocks caught her attention. Dropping to her knees, she peered at it more closely. A spent shell casing! Using a twig, she pried the casing loose then dropped it in an evidence bag. "Good boy, Ozzy!" She pulled the rope toy from her pocket and tossed it for him. He jumped, catching it in his mouth.

Using her radio, she called Meadow. "Ozzy found a brass shell casing."

"That's great news. Grace hasn't alerted at all over here."

Ashley took a moment to peer down at the ranch house. This could very well be where the shooter had been last night. The distance was roughly one hundred and fifty yards. Not difficult for an experienced hunter. Although she felt certain most hunters, especially someone choosing to fire at a pair of cops like her and Ozzy, would have picked up their brass. "We're near the top of the hill and this is the only place Ozzy has alerted. That makes me think he alerted on the scent of gunpowder rather than the man who wore the glove."

"You could be right about that. Yet we both know the shell casing could have been left by a hunter in the area." Meadow was only saying what Chase would when she presented the find.

"I know." Ashley doubted Cade would allow hunters this close to the ranch, but the casing alone didn't prove anything. "Since you and Grace haven't found anything, we can head back."

"Agree. See you down at the ranch." Meadow disconnected from the radio transmission.

Ashley took another few minutes to reward Ozzy for a job well done before heading back. The trip down didn't take nearly as long, and soon she and Ozzy met up with Meadow and Grace.

"What do you think?" Ashley lifted the evidence bag. "I know it could be from any hunter, except for being so close to the ranch house."

"It's worth checking for prints," Meadow agreed. She glanced at her watch. "Sorry, I need to hit the road. Let me know if you need anything else, though."

"Thanks." Ashley headed inside, leaving Meadow and Grace to return to their SUV. She wasn't sure what to make of the fact that Ozzy hadn't alerted on any other areas. The shooter would have had to climb up to that location, and doing so would have left a scent trail. Unless he'd taken some path from higher up?

She went inside, surprised to find Cade at the stove, browning meat. "I thought you wanted to go out for lunch?" She really wanted to interview Melissa's coworkers.

"Hey." He shot her a quick smile over his shoulder. "We are, this is for dinner. Spaghetti okay with you?"

"Um, sure." Flustered by the domestic scene, she filled Ozzy's water dish then took off his vest. Nora had suggested she stick close, protecting Cade and Danny while still working the case. She was only now realizing what a balancing act this was. She wanted to protect them, without getting too close. If that were even possible. She cleared her throat, striving to sound casual. "I'll finish browning the meat if you want to head out to the barn."

"You sure?" His gaze was hopeful.

"Positive." She nudged him aside. "Go ahead. I can manage spaghetti."

"Thanks." Cade nodded at Danny. "I appreciate your help. He should be okay for a couple of hours yet."

"No worries. Ozzy needs to rest, too."

Cade's glance dropped to the evidence bag sticking partially out of her pocket. "He found something?"

"A shell casing." She arched a brow. "You don't allow hunters so close to the house, do you?"

"Never. It's not good hunting land, either. The better place to hunt is ten miles down the road, where the woods are thick and dense." He scowled and washed his hands. "That casing must have been left by the shooter."

Since that's what she also believed, Ashley gave a noncommittal nod as she stepped up to the stove. "Do you think we can leave by noon or so?" As the hour was already eleven fifteen, she understood she wasn't giving him much time.

"I'll make it work." Cade bent to place a quick kiss on Danny's head, then shrugged into his sheepskin coat, placed his brown Stetson firmly on his head, and headed outside.

Cade wasn't like the younger cowboys she'd briefly dated, especially her previous boyfriend, Mike Stucky, who'd cheated on her. Maybe because Cade had the responsibility of the ranch weighing on his shoulders. But his lack of arrogance, and his serious demeanor was a refreshing change.

If she had to be stuck guarding someone, she was glad it was him. Yet she still wished she could be more involved in the task force. Nora had made it clear, with Chase's blessing, that she needed to work the kidnapping case. She silently hoped and prayed she'd be successful in finding Melissa.

The time seemed to drag by, even with the tasks of finishing the spaghetti sauce and cleaning the kitchen, giving her an appreciation for how Cade must be feeling. No doubt he was frustrated by not being able to take care of things the way he normally would.

Danny woke up crying at a quarter after twelve. She had just finished giving him his bottle when Cade returned. A look of concern darkened his green eyes. "Oh, sorry. I should have come earlier."

"It's fine." She grinned. "Changing and feeding Danny wasn't as difficult as I'd imagined." She glanced at Ozzy stretched out at her feet. The dog had followed her as she'd carried Danny to the sofa to change him, as if knowing he was on protection detail, too.

"It seems like Danny is on a three-to-four-hour schedule, which makes things a little easier." He quickly washed up at the sink. "Good timing, too. We should be able to talk to Melissa's coworkers and eat lunch without being interrupted."

"We?" She frowned. "I'll take the lead on interviewing them, Cade." She held Danny to her shoulder, rubbing his back the way Cade had. For someone who hadn't given much thought to having a family of her own, she found caring for the child sweetly humbling. Such a small baby, and so vulnerable. It made her more determined than ever to catch the guy in the ski mask.

"Ready to go?" Cade lifted Danny from her arms, a smile creasing his features. "I'll get him tucked into his snowsuit."

Her heart thumped at the sight of the big tough rancher smiling at the baby. She averted her gaze, reminding herself to remain professional.

Bad enough that Chase didn't trust her with a task force assignment, he'd flip a lid if he knew of this inappropriate attraction to the man she was tasked with protecting.

Ten minutes later, they were in her SUV, with Ozzy in his rear compartment. Once they arrived in Elk Valley, she made her way to the Rusty Spoke. She knew where it was located, although it wasn't her go-to place. There was another family-friendly restaurant in town that she preferred.

She left one of the windows open an inch for Ozzy's sake. The SUV was set up with automatic temperature controls, to make sure her partner was comfortable. She'd rather take him inside, but some restaurants were fussy about allowing pets.

Ozzy was a K-9 officer, but that argument didn't always sway restaurant owners. It was the main reason she preferred the Garden Grove Family Restaurant. The owner hadn't blinked when she'd brought Ozzy in with her.

Cade put Danny's car seat into the stroller. Inside the Rusty Spoke, she noticed several tables were full. They obviously did good business, which was hopefully a testament to their food.

"Seat yourself." A short young woman with dark hair, wearing jeans and a long sleeved Western-style shirt, waved at them. "I'll be over shortly."

"Jessie Baldwin?" Ashley asked nodding toward the retreating back of their server.

"Yep." Cade snagged an empty table, tucking Danny's stroller closer so it would be out of the way. "It might be difficult for her to answer questions since they seem rather busy."

"If she can provide additional names for me to work with, that will be good enough for now."

Less than five minutes later, Jessie approached. "Cade,

it's nice to see you again," She bent to see the baby. "Danny is so sweet." Her expression turned serious. "I heard about Melissa. It's awful."

"Thanks." Cade gestured to her. "This is Officer Ashley Hanson with the Elk Valley PD. She was hoping to talk to you about Melissa."

"Oh, really?" Jessie turned toward her. "What do you need?"

"When was the last time you saw Melissa?"

"Right after Danny was born." Jessie gestured to the sleeping baby. "I stopped by the ranch. Cade was out working in the barn. I brought a chicken-broccoli casserole."

Cade nodded. "I remember. It was very good, thanks."

"That was nice of you," Ashley said. "Do you know if Melissa was seeing anyone recently? Say, in the last week or two?" She carefully gauged the young woman's reaction.

"Like a guy? No." Jessie vehemently shook her head. "She was done with men after the way Vincent up and left town to avoid paying child support." She snorted. "Although his friend, Rafe Travon, may know where Vincent is, if you're looking for him."

Ashley filed that bit of information away. "What about other friends she may have gone out with?"

"Danny is only a month old and she hasn't been off the ranch except for a doctor's appointment." Jessie glanced over as another patron waved at her. "Sorry, are you ready to order?"

"Yes, thanks." They placed their order, and Jessie hurried off to get them water and soft drinks.

"Not as helpful as you'd hoped," he said with a sigh.

"We can look into Rafe Travon." She shrugged. "But I was hoping for more."

The door of the restaurant opened and a tall, beautiful woman with long, red, wavy hair came in. She caught Ashley's attention because she wore carefully applied makeup, along with a long, thick, white-wool coat. She seemed out of place amid the cowboys and ranchers. In fact, she didn't seem to fit into Elk Valley at all.

Danny began to fuss, so Cade quickly bent and lifted the baby from the stroller. He removed the pointy blue hat and opened the snowsuit. "What's the matter, big guy?" He stood swaying back and forth to soothe the infant.

"Cade! How nice to see you!" The stunning redhead strode quickly to their table, her heels clicking on the wooden floor. She wrapped her arms around Cade, giving him a hug and a kiss on the cheek.

Annoyance darkened Cade's eyes and he took a step back, putting distance between them. Ashley watched the exchange with interest, curious about their relationship. "Elaine." Cade's voice held a frosty note. "What brings you to the Rusty Spoke?"

"I heard about Melissa. What can I do to help?" Elaine gazed up at Cade with an expression of devout concern.

"Nothing. Thanks anyway." There was no mistaking the dismissive note in his voice as he dropped into his seat. Ashley could tell he wasn't happy to see Elaine.

"I'm here if you need me." Elaine rested her hand on Cade's arm. He reached over to open Danny's snowsuit, effectively ending the physical contact between them.

It wasn't until Elaine left as quickly as she'd arrived that Ashley realized the woman hadn't so much as looked at Danny. Well, Elaine hadn't paid any attention to Ashley, either, but it was the lack of emotion around Danny that she found oddly disturbing. Not just because Danny was adorable, but because the woman was clearly interested in Cade on a personal level. Wouldn't cooing over the baby be a way to get into his good graces?

The strange interaction convinced her there was more to this story.

One she needed to hear from Cade. Very soon.

SIX

Irritated with Elaine's familiar greeting, hugging and kissing his cheek as if they were still together, Cade worked hard to relax his tense muscles. Glancing at Ashley, he saw the unspoken question in her eyes.

Knowing she deserved an explanation, he sighed and cradled Danny against his chest. "That was Elaine Jurgen. We were engaged, but not any longer."

"Your decision, obviously," Ashley said with a nod.

Startled, he frowned. "No. Actually, it was her choice. She was not happy when I convinced Melissa to live at the ranch permanently. I knew it would be the best place to raise Danny, especially after Vince moved out of town. Elaine threw a fit, ranting and raving about why they would have to live with us after we were married. She tossed my ring in my face and stormed out. Months later, she called and seemed to act as if nothing had happened, hinting we should get together. It made me wonder if she'd expected me to run after her to patch things up." A reluctant smile tweaked the corner of his mouth. "I didn't."

Her eyebrows hiked up. "She probably realized she made a big mistake in letting you go. Yet I'm having trouble understanding why she would have a problem with your family living at your family ranch."

Hearing Ashley's blunt assessment made him realize how unreasonable Elaine's anger had been. His annoyance dissipated. "She also complained when I worked long hours.

Running a ranch by myself isn't easy. I do hire cowboys during the busiest months, but not year-round." Although now that he'd said the words, he realized he might need to consider that plan sooner than later. His main priority was to help find Melissa and care for Danny. But once Melissa was home, having more help might be good, too. Danny was growing and changing daily, and Cade realized he didn't want to miss spending time with his nephew. "It became obvious that Elaine wanted to be a rancher's wife, without the hard work that comes with the title."

"I see." Ashley's eyes held his. "You do realize she didn't look at Danny, not once. It was as if the baby was invisible to her."

Thinking back over their brief and extremely uncomfortable interaction, he realized she was right. "Yeah."

Ashley leaned forward and propped her elbows on the table. "Do you think it's at all possible Elaine has something to do with Melissa's kidnapping? From where I'm sitting, it seems like she has a reason to want Melissa and Danny out of the picture."

"What?" He instinctively shook his head. "No, I can't believe that. Elaine might be self-centered and high-maintenance, but labeling her a criminal seems extreme."

She didn't relent. "Think about it. You just told me that she broke things off because Melissa and Danny were planning to live with you indefinitely. Could be she thinks she'll have another chance with you if they're gone."

His jaw dropped as her words sank in. Was Ashley right? Could it be that Elaine would stoop so low as to pull a stunt like this? It was an outlandish theory, yet he had gotten the sense that her concern over Melissa's kidnapping was fake. Especially considering how angry she had been at the idea of Melissa and Danny living with them after the wedding. Looking back at how much Elaine had changed over time, he wondered if he'd ever known the real woman. Maybe she'd created a fake persona to impress him, going back to her real self over time.

Was everything about her fake? Including her so-called love for him? Probably.

But, kidnapping? Taking a woman and a baby against their will? To do what? Get rid of them forever? Icy fingers of fear trailed down his spine.

"It's a possibility we have to investigate." Ashley's voice was low but firm.

"I see your point." As much as he hated to admit it, she was right about investigating all possibilities. Even if to eliminate Elaine as a suspect. "You're the cop, Ashley. I agree you need to investigate all angles. But I doubt Elaine would get her fingers dirty doing the work herself. She also isn't able to shoot a gun. At least, not accurately."

"Good to know. Though she easily could have hired someone. Where does she work?"

"The Elk Valley Chateau. At the front desk." He shook his head helplessly. "Not the résumé of a kidnapper."

Yet he hated to admit it was possible. Melissa had never cared much for Elaine, making her feelings known by calling her "high maintenance." To be fair, he'd said some derogatory things about Vincent, too, so he hadn't thought too much about Melissa's concerns. Elaine liked to spend money on fancy clothes, makeup and jewelry. But didn't most women enjoy that kind of thing?

Now he wondered if Melissa had been on to something. A flash of anger hit hard at the possibility of Elaine being involved in this. He curled his fingers into fists, holding himself in check. If Elaine was responsible, he would make sure she was prosecuted to the full extent of the law.

His thoughts were interrupted by the arrival of their meals. It wasn't easy, but he shoved his anger aside and reached across the table to take Ashley's hand. "I'll say grace."

"Of course." Ashley bowed her head.

"Dear Lord Jesus, we are grateful for this meal You've provided to us. We ask that You keep Melissa and Danny safe in Your loving care and that you guide Ashley to the truth. Amen."

"Amen," Ashley echoed. She lifted her head and smiled. "That was nice, Cade."

He nodded, releasing her hand. He wanted to believe Ashley's care and concern was real and honest. In his heart, he didn't believe Ashley was anything like Elaine.

But he'd been fooled once. He wasn't about to allow himself to be vulnerable, again. Ashley was young and, these days, he felt positively ancient. Safer to keep his distance, despite the sizzling attraction.

"We shouldn't linger." He dug into his meal. "Ozzy is probably wondering where you are. I don't like that he's outside."

"He'll be okay. The SUV has a temperature-control sensor." Ashley smiled. "It would have been interesting to see Ozzy's reaction to Elaine. I don't think she's the one who actually kidnapped your sister, or dropped the glove, but he's a pretty good judge of character."

He couldn't hold back a wry smile. "I'm sure he'll take an instant dislike to her."

She laughed softly. "Maybe. Knowing she works at the Elk Valley Chateau helps. I'll stop in to chat with her again, very soon."

He ate quickly, eyeing the time. It wouldn't be long until Danny would be ready for another bottle. Planning his day around the baby's schedule wasn't easy, but he would do whatever was necessary to care for his nephew until Ashley found Melissa. He had faith in the K-9 team's ability.

There was no doubt in his mind that Ashley and Ozzy would uncover the truth. And when they did, he'd be more than a little satisfied to see whomever had taken his sister put behind bars.

When their lunch was over, Ashley led the way outside. "Do you mind if I make another stop at the precinct?"

"Not at all." Cade strapped in Danny's car seat with the seat belt. The baby made noises, not a full outcry, but enough to indicate he was getting hungry. "I'll have to feed him soon."

"I want to update my chief and task force team leader with my new theory about Elaine, and we need to find this Rafe Travon guy, too." Ashley could manage the conversation via phone, but wanted to see their respective reactions. She thought Elaine was a viable suspect, but wasn't sure if Chase or Nora would feel the same way.

"I understand." If Cade was upset at the delay in getting back to the ranch, he didn't show it. "I'll fill his bottle when we get there."

"Sounds good. I'm sure this won't take too long." She smiled at Ozzy in the rearview mirror. Her K-9 partner seemed to grin back at her.

Less than five minutes later, she pulled up in front of the police station. She decided to take Ozzy in with her, since he'd been cooped up for a while. Cade brought Danny in, too, disappearing down the hallway to the restrooms where he could access warm water.

When she crossed to Nora's office, her steps slowed as she realized an older couple was walking through the doorway, heading toward her, their faces etched with sorrow. She recognized them as Aaron Anderson's parents. Aaron had been one of the three original murder victims killed ten years ago. His mother sniffled and looked at Ozzy. Her

K-9 partner was wearing his work vest, but his tail wagged in greeting, as he generally liked people.

"Such a sweet boy," Aaron's mother whispered, gazing longingly at Ozzy.

"He is," Aaron's father agreed.

"Ah, thank you. He's a working dog, my K-9 partner." If Ozzy wasn't on duty, she'd have invited them to pet him. Unfortunately, he was wearing his vest, so she didn't. It occurred to her that an emotional support dog would be helpful as the task force navigated this investigation. As the grieving couple moved past, she made a mental note to ask Chase about the possibility.

"What's up?" Nora queried, looking exhausted. "Please tell me you have good news."

Ashley brought her chief up to date on the interaction between Elaine Jurgen and Cade. Thankfully, her boss seemed interested in her theory. "Good observation. Go ahead and dig into her background a bit."

"I will, thanks. We also need to talk to a guy named Rafe Travon. He was good friends with Melissa's ex-boyfriend, Vincent Orr, and we believe he could be helping him in some way. I know Orr has left town, and we should talk to him, too. It may be easier to grab Travon first, if he's still in the area."

"I agree. Hold on a minute." Nora worked the keyboard. Despite her role as chief of police, Nora didn't delegate tasks she could easily perform herself. She jotted information on a sticky note and handed it to her. "Here's Travon's last-known address. If he's not there, we can issue a BOLO as a person of interest."

"Great. Isla put together a search warrant for Vincent's financial records. Did the judge sign off?"

"No, there's no proof that Vincent is involved. Especially

since Ozzy didn't alert at the apartment over the garage."
Nora sighed. "You're better off trying to find Rafe Travon."

"Okay, I can swing by and see what I can uncover." The
news was disappointing, but she understood. Ashley tucked
the note in her pocket and gestured at the door. "I saw the
Andersons leave. They looked upset."

Nora gave a solemn nod. "The entire town is on edge
with the news of these two recent murders. Even though
the victims were found in other Rocky Mountain states,
they both grew up in Elk Valley and were members of the
Young Rancher's Club."

Ashley nodded. "Is Agent Rawlston still around?" She
wanted to ask him about the emotional support dog. "I
thought I'd update him, too."

"He's taken over the conference room."

"Thanks." Ashley headed there next, passing Cade cra-
dling Danny in the crook of his arm as he gave him a bottle. Seeing the tough rancher with the sweet baby made her
breath catch. Cade was all about working hard while also
dedicating his life to his family. A trait she found incredibly endearing, maybe because of her absentee father. Giving herself a mental shake, she turned away.

Chase was in the conference room, on his cell phone.
She hovered in the doorway, waiting for him to finish. He
didn't appear overly happy to see her, but gave her a nod
of acknowledgment after ending the call. "What's up?"

She succinctly filled him in on her theory of Elaine Jurgen being involved in the kidnapping, along with her intent
to track down Rafe Travon as a known associate of Vincent
Orr's. Much like Nora, he didn't dismiss her concern, but
nodded. "Sounds like you have several good lines to tug.
Is there something you need from me?" His voice wasn't
impatient, but she sensed he wanted to move on with whatever he was working on.

"I think we need an emotional support dog. Certain breeds of dogs, much like your golden retriever, Dash, have been shown to soothe and comfort those in distress. The town is being forced to relive these murders, and I just saw one of the victim's families leaving the chief's office. They're going to need help to get through this."

Chase frowned, as he stroked Dash's fur. "I don't have the funds for that, but you are welcome to run this past your father. He's the one with the financial juice to get something like that approved."

She hesitated, wishing she'd taken more time to think this through. The last thing she wanted was for Chase to believe she always ran to her dad for favors. Yet, the distressed features on Aaron's parents' faces were clearly embedded in her mind. She truly believed dogs could be therapeutic in healing wounds. Weren't the victims more important than her ego? She reluctantly nodded. "Yeah, okay. I can do that."

"Let me know how it goes. Do you need anything else?" Chase glanced at the door, clearly indicating their time was finished.

"Since the task force is sharing some resources with the police department, I was hoping you might have some information from the glove, boot print or shell casing." She glanced at him as she walked toward the door.

"DNA will take some time," Chase pointed out. "Hopefully we'll know more about the shell casing and boot print, soon. The task force was set up to find the killer, but I've agreed to work with Nora and to share our resources. If we get a hot lead, though, your intel may take a back seat."

"I understand. Thanks. And I'll keep you updated on how things go with Rafe Travon." She stepped through the doorway and reached for her phone. Since Cade was still feeding Danny, she made the call to her father.

"Ashley, how are you?" Brian Hanson's voice boomed over the connection. "How are things with the task force?"

"Great." She would not complain about her sidelined role. "But I need some help, Dad. The victims' families are reliving the nightmare from ten years ago. I was wondering if the FBI would approve an emotional support dog for us."

"An emotional support dog?" Ashley wished she could read her father's features. Was he smirking at her proposal? Or was he seriously considering it? "Not a bad idea. I'll see what I can do."

She let out her breath in a soundless sigh. "Thanks, Dad. Keep me posted, okay?"

"Sure, sure." She heard a phone ringing in the background. "I need to take that, Ashley. Go get the bad guys."

Before she could respond, her father disconnected from the call. She tucked her phone in her pocket, hoping he'd taken her request seriously. Her dad didn't have much of a touchy-feely side. His job with the Bureau was everything to him, and even when she was growing up, he'd often brushed off her requests. She made a note to remind him about the idea if he didn't get back to her soon.

"Cade, would you stay here for a few minutes?" She smiled when Ozzy nudged the baby with his velvet nose. "I need to drive past an address. Shouldn't take too long."

"That's fine, anything that helps find Melissa. I do need to get back to the ranch soon, though." He looked incredibly weary for a moment. "I still have chores to do."

"I know. I'll be quick." She led Ozzy outside to the SUV. After putting him in back, she quickly slid behind the wheel. She didn't need to pull the note from her pocket. She was familiar with the apartment building, she'd once lived there herself. It was located three blocks off Main Street.

The place looked exactly the same as when she'd lived

there, down to the broken lock on the main door. The building wasn't known for its high level security. Rafe lived in apartment three, so she buzzed the door.

No answer.

She tried again, but there was still no response. Since she knew Orville Granger, the manager, she buzzed his door.

"Whaddya want?" His cranky voice made her smile.

"It's Ashley Hanson. Can I talk to you for a minute?"

He heaved a sigh. "Yeah, come on down."

She headed to apartment one, with Ozzy at her heels. The door opened before she could knock.

Orville's white hair was mostly gone, except for tufts that stuck out around his ears. Despite his perpetual grouchiness, she smiled fondly. "I've missed you, Orv."

"Humph." His gaze dropped to the dog. "He better not make a mess."

"He won't." Looking over Orv's shoulder, she noticed his apartment was just as disorganized and full of stuff as ever. "I won't keep you long, but I need to know where I can find Rafe Travon."

"Who?" Orv looked confused.

"Rafe Travon," she repeated in a loud voice, in case the manager's hearing was going. "He lives in apartment three."

"Oh, him." Orv snorted. "He don't live here anymore."

"Since when?" A flicker of anticipation hit hard.

"Three months ago. He didn't pay his rent, so I put up an eviction notice. Next day, I used the master key to get inside. The place was empty." Orv scowled. "At least he didn't steal the appliances."

"Three months ago, huh?" She wondered if that was when the kidnapping plan had been hatched. Then again, Danny was only one month old. In truth, it would have been easier to kidnap Melissa when she was pregnant rather than wait for her to have the baby.

"Why are ya lookin' for him?" Orv stared at her. "Ya going to arrest him?"

"I just want to talk to him, that's all." The last thing Ashley wanted was for the rumor mill to run away with the idea that Rafe was guilty of something. It didn't take much to get tongues wagging. "I take it he didn't leave a forwarding address?"

"Nah." Orv waved a hand. "He wouldn't risk me tracking him down to get the money he owed me." The old man abruptly brightened. "You lookin' for a place to live? I already have someone in his place, but I got another one available. There's an extra monthly fee for pets, though."

"Sorry, but I'm fine in my small house. Thanks anyway." She liked having a backyard for Ozzy to run in, even if it was the size of a postage stamp. She dug a business card out of her pocket. "Orv, would you call me if Rafe shows up again? He's not in trouble," she hastened to add. "I just want to talk to him."

He took the card, shaking his head. "I'm tellin' ya, he ain't gonna come back. Not when he owes me money."

"Just in case he does. Thanks." She stepped back, anxious now to get back to Cade and Danny. "Take care of yourself."

"Yeah, yeah," he muttered before shutting his door.

Ashley pulled her phone to call the dispatcher. "I need a BOLO put out on a Rafe Travon. He's a person of interest in the kidnapping."

"Understood, consider it done," the dispatcher responded.

As she hung up, she received a call from Cade. "I, uh, need to get back to the ranch. Danny threw up on my shirt."

"Be there in a jiffy." She quickened her pace leading Ozzy outside. She made the trip back to the station in less than five minutes.

Cade was hovering by the front door. The moment she pulled up, he stepped out, carrying Danny's car seat. His rawhide coat was open, revealing a dark stain on the right upper portion of his dark green Western shirt.

Once Cade had Danny buckled in, he slid in beside her. "I hope I didn't interrupt your work."

"You didn't." She considered how much to tell him. "I didn't find Rafe Travon. He's been gone for three months. We've issued a BOLO for him, though. Hopefully, he's still in Elk Valley."

"I hope you can find him and soon." Cade scowled as he stared down at the stain on his shirt. "It's my fault. I know I'm supposed to use a rag to cover my clothes."

She bit her lip to keep from smiling. "At least he didn't get your coat."

"There's that," Cade agreed.

She navigated the SUV through town, heading for the highway that would take them to Cade's ranch. The main task she still needed to complete was to comb through Melissa's phone records. Isla had sent her the reports, and she wanted to review each of the recent phone calls for herself.

It was possible the abductor had called her phone to entice her into leaving the ranch. Unless he'd gotten her to come outside under her own power. Either way, she had to believe there would be a clue within the records. Another line to tug, as Chase had said.

"Hey, there's a black minivan." Cade's voice broke into her thoughts.

"Where?" Then she saw it up ahead, turning onto another highway. It looked to be similar to the one that had taken Melissa away from Elk Valley Park.

"Hurry," Cade urged. "Don't let him get away."

She couldn't drive recklessly with Cade, Danny and

Ozzy in the SUV, but increased her speed as much as she dared.

The minivan disappeared around a curve.

"Don't let him get away," Cade urged.

She turned the corner, desperate to catch up with the vehicle. This could be the break they needed.

Especially if Rafe Travon was behind the wheel.

SEVEN

Keeping his eyes glued to the minivan, Cade's heart thumped in his chest. Was Melissa inside the van? Was this the moment they'd find her?

"Can you make out the license plate?" Ashley asked.

"I'm trying." He squinted and focused on the tag. As she shortened the distance between them, he realized the plate wasn't covered by mud. "I can make out the letters and numbers now. It's TR4952."

"I'll call it in." Ashley had both of her hands on the wheel, but used her thumb to activate the hands-free functionality. "This is Unit 7. I need a license plate run."

Seconds later, the dispatcher responded. "Ten-four, Unit 7. What's the number?"

Ashley glanced at him, so he repeated the information for the dispatcher.

"Ten-four, one moment please." The dispatcher paused for a moment. They were closer to the minivan now. Oddly, the van wasn't attempting to escape them.

Was this the wrong vehicle? The hope that had blossomed in his chest withered.

"Unit 7, that vehicle is registered to a Sam Jones out of Laramie. I did a quick background check. He appears to be an engineer working for the power company. He has a wife, Amy, and they've been married for two years. No evidence of any criminal activity or financial troubles. I don't think you have probable cause to pull them over. There are dozens of black vans in the state of Wyoming."

"Thanks, Dispatch. Appreciate the information."

Ashley disconnected from the call then pressed down on the accelerator to pass the minivan on the left. Cade turned to look at the young couple inside, who seemed completely oblivious to their speedy approach.

"It's probably not the van used to kidnap Melissa." He couldn't hide his keen disappointment. "I had hoped…"

"I know." Ashley reached out to rest her hand on his arm. "I'm sorry, Cade. But we have several leads to follow. We're going to find her."

"Yeah." He knew Ashley would do everything in her power to make that happen. He wanted to believe Melissa hadn't been harmed, that the kidnapper was holding her until he or she had grabbed Danny.

But there was no guarantee. Especially if the goal was to get rid of them both.

Elaine? He hadn't wanted to believe it, but as he'd cared for Danny in the police station while waiting for Ashley, the possibility had swirled in his mind. He'd replayed the way Elaine had approached at the Rusty Spoke, hugging and kissing his cheek. The way she'd gazed up at him with wide eyes. She'd seemed like the woman he'd dated and ultimately asked to marry him. Now, the fake concern over his sister had seemed so obvious. He was working hard to keep the ranch afloat, but that wasn't a good excuse not to have clued in to Elaine's real personality. He was ashamed to admit he'd gotten himself engaged to her in the first place.

Elaine had wanted him, not because of who he was as a man, but because of the prestige of being a rancher's wife and maybe even to have access to his money. He remembered the one time he'd taken her shopping for her birthday. She'd spent several hundred dollars without blinking an eye.

He hadn't protested, but maybe he should have. Like most people, she didn't realize many ranches were resource rich, meaning plenty of cattle and other livestock, but cash poor.

Thank goodness for Melissa and Danny, who'd thrown a wrench in Elaine's plan. Her tossing his ring back had been the best thing that had happened to him.

Painful to think Elaine may have been so coldly calculating in her efforts to win him back that she'd come up with this desperate kidnapping scheme. As if the minute Melissa and Danny were gone, he'd just fall into her arms.

Never, he thought darkly.

Ashley slowed the SUV and made a U-turn at the next intersection to head to the ranch. He twisted in his seat to check on Danny, glad he was sleeping.

Stifling a yawn of his own, he hoped to have time to finish some chores before the baby needed to be fed again. It had been difficult to sit at the police station while knowing the work that waited for him at home.

"I've been thinking about the possibility of Elaine having a role in this…" He kept his voice even.

"You still care about her." It wasn't a question.

"No!" He almost yelled the word then winced at how he could have woken Danny. "I don't. She was different when we first met, but looking back, it's easy to see I never should have dated her, much less asked her to marry me. That was the worst lapse of judgment, ever."

"Hey, we all make mistakes." Ashley's smile vanished. "Different how?"

"She didn't complain about the hours I spent working. Seemed to like being out on the ranch, but then would say something derogatory about cow dung on my boots." He flushed. "Ranching isn't always neat and clean. The longer we were together, the more negative she became. But that's a far cry from doing something this drastic. Kidnapping my sister and nephew, an innocent baby?" He shook his head. "Did she think I wouldn't grieve over losing them? Or rest until I'd gotten to the bottom of what happened to them?"

"Maybe she planned to be your support during that difficult time." Ashley shrugged. "Manipulative people believe they can do anything and get away with it."

That description fit Elaine to a tee. Maybe she hadn't changed so much as she had allowed her true nature to come through, giving up the pretense. The thought gave him a chill.

"Is there anything else you can tell me about Elaine? Does she have any family members who could be working for her?"

Ashley's question was a good one. He wanted to do his part to find Melissa. "Yes, she has a younger brother, Joe. He's out on the cowboy circuit, though, so I'm not sure where he is now. Last I heard, he was in Montana somewhere. Elaine and her brother weren't very close. The rodeo season won't start until late May, that's when he's usually in this area." He wished he'd thought to mention her brother sooner.

"Joe Jurgen?" Ashley pursed her lips. "I'll start digging into his background after I review Melissa's phone records."

"Okay." He was glad there was another avenue to investigate. He wanted to take her hand, but he could see the entry to the McNeal Four Ranch up ahead so he held back. "Thanks, Ashley."

"We'll find her, Cade." Her encouraging smile warmed his heart. The care and concern she expressed came across as genuine and helped him feel grounded, too. As if there was nothing they couldn't accomplish by working together.

"We will." He infused confidence in his tone. God's strength and wisdom would get him and Danny through this.

"I know you have things to do," Ashley said as she took

the long winding driveway toward the ranch house. "I'll watch Danny while you take care of chores. I can work on my laptop in between feedings."

"That would be great, thank you." Her willingness to pitch in was humbling. "There's a section of fence I really need to repair or risk losing cattle. It shouldn't take too long."

"No problem." She stopped the SUV near the garage and shut down the engine. "I need a few minutes to let Ozzy out first, then you're free to go."

"Sounds good." He unbuckled Danny's car seat and carried his nephew inside, leaving Ashley and Ozzy to do their thing. He changed Danny's diaper and his one-piece sleeper, which was also stained from when the baby threw up. Lastly, he carried Danny into his bedroom so he also could change his own shirt.

By the time he emerged, Ashley and Ozzy were in the kitchen. He set Danny's infant seat on the table, noting the baby's eyes were open. He couldn't help grinning at the boy. "You're awake, huh, big guy?"

Danny turned his dark eyes toward the sound of his voice. Was it possible the baby was already tuning in to his surroundings? Or was it his imagination?

"No sign of trouble outside," Ashley said as she set her laptop on the other side of the kitchen table. "I had Ozzy do a quick sniff around the ranch house to be sure Glove Guy hadn't been nearby."

"Good." He reached for his rawhide coat, resetting his Stetson on his head. He nodded toward the kitchen counter. "I have a bottle ready to be made in case you need it while I'm gone. I'll also have my phone, so please don't hesitate to call if you need me."

"Understood." She gave him a long look. "Be careful,

Cade. I know the kidnapper was probably trying to grab Danny, but I want you to be on alert for possible danger."

"I'll have my rifle." He lifted the gun and slung the strap over his shoulder, touched by her concern. "If Elaine is behind this, I doubt she'll want me dead."

"True. But if someone hired Rafe Travon to do the kidnapping, he might eliminate you if you get in his way," Ashley pointed out. "That also goes for Joe Jurgen."

He nodded, conceding the point. "I'll be careful. You, too."

"Ozzy, Danny and I will be fine."

He hesitated at the doorway, fighting a strange reluctance to leave. Giving himself a mental shake, he walked outside, closing the door behind him.

Striding toward the barn, he forced himself to stay focused on the work that needed to be done, like repairing the fence. He needed to take advantage of the few hours he had to complete the most important chores.

Imagining what his life might be like with a woman like Ashley at his side was a useless endeavor. Chores and finding Melissa were his priority.

Not this sudden and acute sense of loneliness.

Ashley quickly got to work, not knowing how long she'd have until Danny needed her attention. Melissa's phone records landed in her email, so she went through those first. Starting with the most recent calls and working backward, she painstakingly recorded the handful of numbers. One specific number had called Melissa's phone several times over the past two days before her disappearance. It had a different area code and, after digging further, she wasn't surprised to discover it was a burner phone purchased with cash in Cheyenne. When she tried to call the number, it was no longer in use.

Hoping there was a video camera at the store where it had been purchased, Ashley made several calls. When she reached the manager, he informed her the camera hadn't been working for the past three weeks. She requested all video feeds for the two months prior to when the camera had failed, and he grudgingly agreed to send them to her.

For the moment, she'd reached a dead end. The other numbers belonged to Jessie Baldwin, the land line at the Rusty Spoke, Vincent Orr and Cade.

It was interesting that the last call on Melissa's phone had with Vincent was over three months before Danny had been born. Her ex-boyfriend had left Elk Valley earlier than that, so Ashley found it curious they'd been in communication. She took a moment to find his new address. Unfortunately, his driver's license still carried the old address of Elk Valley. And there was no evidence that Vincent had signed a new lease, either. He was either living in his car or with friends. Likely the latter. No doubt working for cash to avoid child support, too.

She rubbed her temples and decided to switch gears. Time to dig into Elaine and Joe Jurgen.

Before she could type Elaine's name in the search engine, her phone rang. Her father's name flashed on the screen.

"Hi, Dad." She stood and moved into the living room, Ozzy at her heels, so she wouldn't wake Danny.

"Ashley, I wanted to let you know that I think the emotional support dog is a great idea. The upper brass turned down your request, but I've made arrangements for a sweet labradoodle pup named Cowgirl to be gifted to Rawlston's task force."

"You paid for the dog?" She wasn't sure she'd heard him correctly.

"Yes, I did. You know I'll do anything for my girl." She

winced at the endearment he'd used so often while being hundreds of miles away from her and her mother. Giving gifts had been his MO, rather than spending time with her. "The pup is one year old and will be arriving within the next few days. I thought you'd want to be the one to tell Rawlston the good news."

Why, so I can ingratiate myself to him? Hope this will help him let go of his resentment to my presence on his task force?

She winced at the uncharitable thought. No sense reiterating her annoyance with her dad's interfering with her professional life. It went against the grain to accept personal favors from her father, especially knowing it had been Chase's idea for her to ask him in the first place. But for this, she decided to make an exception. Not for her, but for those victims who would benefit from interacting with Cowgirl.

"Thanks, Dad. This is wonderful news." She hoped he didn't notice the forced enthusiasm in her tone. "I'll let Chase know. He'll want our K-9 trainer, Liana Lightfoot, involved in Cowgirl's care."

"Great! How is the case coming along?"

"Chase has handed out various assignments, and everyone is hard at work." The last thing she wanted was for him to know she hadn't been given anything to do. "Speaking of which, I need to get back to work myself. Thanks again for arranging for Cowgirl. I know she'll be a great addition to the team."

"Keep me updated on your progress," her father said. "Take care, Ashley."

"You, too." She disconnected from the call, staring down at Ozzy for a moment. He sat beside her as if sensing her discomfort. She could always trust her K-9 to be there for her.

Unlike her father.

Then again, he had come through with the emotional support dog. Just the thought of a labradoodle pup made her smile. She told herself to let it go and returned to her computer. She spent twenty minutes searching for information on Joe Jurgen. She found his driver's license photo and his last-known address being Cody, Wyoming, which wasn't far from Elk Valley. She was considering the possibility of heading to his place when her phone rang again.

This time, her chief's name lit up the screen. "Hey, Chief. Do you have something for me?"

"Hanson, I wanted you to know an abandoned black Chevy minivan was found five miles outside of town," Nora Quan said. "When the officer cleared the mud from the plate and called it in, they discovered the vehicle wasn't the one you followed earlier, it was stolen from Cheyenne."

Cheyenne again? The connection between the stolen van and the disposable phone was interesting. "Any other leads on the van?"

"No obvious blood, fingerprints, or other evidence was found so far, but we have the crime scene techs combing the vehicle for hairs, prints and fibers."

"What about the glove, rope and heel print? Chase said DNA would take time, but didn't have any other information when I asked."

"Unfortunately, those items haven't given us much to go on," Nora said. "The rope is plain twine and available from our local store, frequently purchased by ranchers. The heel print is from a common hiking boot, estimated to be a men's size ten or eleven. Chase is right about the DNA, we are hopeful the perp left some skin cells behind on the rope and glove."

The shoe size wasn't much, but the van could turn up more forensic evidence. Her gaze landed on the picture on the fireplace mantel of Cade, Melissa and Danny, taken shortly after his birth. Melissa wore her long dark hair in waves around her face. If she had been transported in that van, Ashley felt certain Melissa's hair would be found inside. "That's good, Chief. I hope they can come up with something more soon."

"Me, too." Nora sounded tired. "Nothing new on your end?"

"A burner phone call was the last contact with Melissa's phone before she went missing, and it was purchased in Cheyenne. I'm working on finding Joe Jurgen, he's Elaine's younger brother." Her efforts sounded rather pathetic, even though she knew many cases were cracked because of attention to detail. "Oh, and a female labradoodle puppy has been gifted to the task force as an emotional support dog. She'll be here in a few days."

"We could use her right now," Nora said on a sigh. "I've been meeting with many of the victims' families while Rawlston focuses his attention on the investigation into the murders. Thanks, Hanson. Keep me updated."

"I will." Ashley dropped the phone from her ear to end the call. She found herself silently praying the abandoned black Chevy minivan wouldn't turn out to be another dead end.

After speaking with Jessie at the Rusty Spoke and observing the interaction between Elaine and Cade, she'd felt sure they'd get a lead.

But, so far, she was coming up empty.

Danny woke from his nap. She quickly filled the bottle with warm, but not too hot, water, shaking it to dissolve the formula inside. Then she lifted the crying baby and took him into the living room so she could feed him. Ozzy stretched out at her feet, watching with his dark eyes.

The baby's eyes clung to hers as he quieted. She couldn't

help being enthralled by the miracle of birth and this tiny human. He was perfect in every way, and when his fingers wrapped around her fingertip, her heart melted.

Despite not attending church in years, a Bible verse, Luke 18:16, sprang into her mind. *But Jesus called them unto him, and said, Suffer little children to come unto me, and forbid them not: for of such is the kingdom of God.*

"Jesus is watching over your mommy," she whispered to him. "You'll be together, soon."

When Danny finished his bottle, she lifted him onto her shoulder, mindful to put a rag over it first to protect her uniform shirt. The baby didn't spit up this time, but let out a soft burp.

She stood and carried him to the infant seat. Caring for him was nice, but she needed to keep searching for clues that would get them one step closer to finding Melissa.

Her phone vibrated with an incoming call. The number looked familiar and, after a moment, she realized it was Jessie Baldwin's number, the one she'd recently noted on Melissa's phone records. She quickly answered. "This is Ashley Hanson."

"Officer Hanson? I—um, sorry I couldn't talk to you more earlier, but I'm on break now."

"That's okay, I understand." Her plan to make dinner vanished as she focused on Jessie's voice. "You can call me any time. Did you think of something about Melissa?"

"Yes, that's why I called." The young woman's tone was hesitant. "I don't want to throw anyone under the bus, but I saw Elaine talking to you and Cade at lunch. It reminded me about an argument Elaine had with Melissa while she was still pregnant and working at the restaurant. Maybe four months ago?"

"Argument?" Her pulse spiked. "About what?"

"Melissa claimed that Elaine demanded she move off the ranch so Cade could have a life of his own."

Ashley swallowed a flash of anger. Not that Cade didn't deserve a life of his own, but that Elaine would encourage Melissa to move out of the ranch while pregnant and alone. "I'm sure Melissa didn't appreciate that."

"She was upset," Jessie agreed. "She loves her brother and doesn't want to hold him back. But it's not as if the ranch house isn't big enough for everyone. I told her Elaine was just being selfish. I assured her that Cade wanted her to stay with him and that he was better off without Elaine anyway."

Ashley silently agreed. "Was that the end of the matter?"

"As far as I know. It may not be relevant to your investigation, but I wanted you to be aware."

"Thanks, Jessie. I'm glad you called." She ended the call as the front door opened and Cade walked in. He set the rifle in the corner, but must have read her concern because he crossed over to her.

"What is it? What's wrong?"

"Nothing. Just that Jessie let me know how Elaine cornered Melissa at the Rusty Spoke a few months ago, telling her she needed to move out of the ranch house so you would be free to live your own life."

His green eyes darkened. "How dare she? I never wanted that. I hope Melissa didn't believe her."

"I don't think she did. Jessie pointed out how Elaine was being selfish."

Cade turned away. He hung his coat and hat on the hook by the door then stood with his shoulders slumped.

"Don't," she whispered, coming over to put a hand on his arm. "This isn't your fault."

"Isn't it?" He turned to face her, his expression tortured. "I brought that viper into our lives."

Feeling helpless, Ashley wasn't sure what to say. She wanted to give him some comfort, so she slipped her arm around his waist and hugged him. "Like I said before, we all make mistakes."

"What was your mistake?" His low, husky voice sent shivers of awareness down her spine.

"I dated a guy who cheated on me. I know it wasn't my fault, but I still wished I'd have been smarter about my choices."

"He's an idiot." Cade pulled her closer, hugging her back. "His failures are not yours."

"Just like Elaine's failures aren't yours, either." She glanced up at him. Their eyes locked and held for several beats. She had to force herself to pull away.

Being in Cade's embrace felt right, but crossing the line like this was inviting trouble.

Big trouble.

EIGHT

Cade let Ashley go as Ozzy wedged himself between them. The dog's attempt to separate them was comical, and a blessing in disguise. What was it about her that called to him? She was dedicated to finding Melissa, but he sensed she'd be that way with any case. Maybe he wanted to believe what they shared was more special than it really was.

After everything he'd gone through with Elaine, the last thing he needed or wanted was to get close to Ashley. Holding her wasn't smart, although he'd readily do it again if given the chance.

"I, uh, we should eat dinner." He pushed the sentence past his tight throat. Had he made anything for dinner? His mind went completely blank.

"Yes, but I need to cook the spaghetti noodles, first." Ashley's husky voice was not helping. He took a step forward before he caught himself.

He didn't have time for this. Reuniting Melissa and Danny was his main priority. The thought helped steady him.

"Right." How could he have forgotten the spaghetti? "Sit down. I'll take care of it. You shouldn't have to."

"Okay, I need to feed Ozzy anyway." After a long moment, she turned away to tend to her K-9 partner, shrugging into her coat and taking him outside.

Drawing in a deep breath, he opened the pantry. He stared blankly at the contents for a full thirty seconds before he was able to shake off the impact of their embrace long enough to find the noodles.

Pull yourself together, cowboy, he sternly lectured himself. *Danny needs you. So does Melissa. Stay focused!*

He filled a pan with water and turned on the gas stove. Then he heated up the sauce and meat he'd made earlier. As he worked, Ashley returned with Ozzy's dishes and went about providing food and water.

"Did Danny give you any trouble?" He sent her a quick glance, wishing things between them could get back to normal.

"Not at all." Her eyes darted to the clock. "I gave him a bottle about forty-five minutes ago."

"Thanks for doing that. I know caring for my nephew isn't your job, but I appreciate the assistance."

"I don't mind." Her tone was light, as if she, too, was striving to sound normal. "I was able to get some work done."

"Were you able to find anything helpful on Melissa's case? Other than the audacity of Elaine poking her nose where it didn't belong." The way she'd badgered his sister burned in his belly.

"I have a few leads." Ashley dropped into a kitchen chair with a sigh.

"Anything you can share?" He understood that cops didn't normally give victims' families hourly updates, but in this case, he desperately needed them. "Please? I want to help find her. Danny needs his mother."

She nodded slowly. "Melissa hasn't had any calls from Vincent in the past four months. The last call she received was from a burner phone purchased in Cheyenne. That same burner phone number popped up several times over several days prior to her disappearance, too."

"Can you track it?"

"I tried." She scowled. "Unfortunately, the store's cameras weren't working at the time of the purchase. I requested video feeds prior to that breakdown in case this guy went there earlier."

"If Vincent or Rafe went in to buy other items, can we tie them to the burner phone?"

"Not unless we see them buying one. What I'm hoping for is that one of them purchased it early, but didn't activate and use the device right away. If the camera shows them buying something else?" She shrugged. "Could be considered circumstantial evidence. Especially if Vincent was there, as he allegedly moved out of state."

That made sense. The news was encouraging, but he wanted more. Twenty-four hours had already passed since Melissa's kidnapping. It was killing him to not know where she was, or if she was even alive.

Please, Lord, don't take Melissa from me and Danny. Please protect her and keep her safe!

His silent prayer didn't ease the sick tension in his gut. He'd done his best to focus on ranch chores, but his sister's disappearance was always in the forefront of his mind. What if Vincent was behind this and had taken Melissa out of state? There was no way Ashley and Ozzy could track her there.

Then again, what was Vincent's motive? The guy had skipped town rather than face being a dad and making child support payments.

No, that part didn't make sense. It had to be something else. But what?

"Cade?" Ashley's voice startled him from his reverie.

"What?" He instinctively looked to Danny, but the baby was still sleeping.

"The water is boiling." She gestured to it.

"Oh, yeah." He put the noodles in and stirred. When they were cooked, he removed the pan from the heat and dumped the noodles in a strainer. "Time to eat."

"Great." Ashley came over to join him. He filled two plates with spaghetti and covered them with sauce, handing one to Ashley.

Together, they returned to the table. The cozy intimacy of being there with Ashley and Danny messed with Cade's mind. It was all too easy to imagine having someone special to come home to at the end of each day.

Someone like Ashley?

Whoa, dig in your heels and pull back the reins. Do not go there.

"Cade? Would you like to say grace?"

Again, Ashley's voice pulled him back to reality. He must be in dire need of sleep to have his mind wandering like this. "Of course." He cleared his throat. "Dear Lord Jesus, we thank You for this food we are blessed to eat. We ask that You continue to keep Melissa safe in Your care, and guide Ashley and Ozzy to finding her very soon. Amen."

"I would also ask that You keep Cade safe in Your care, too. Amen," she added.

"Thank you." He stared at his plate for a moment, stunned by how much her prayer meant to him. He'd never been the focus of someone's prayers. At least, not that he'd known about. Melissa had always let him take the lead, rather than participate the way Ashley did. The tightness in his stomach loosened, reinforcing the power of praying for someone else. He didn't deserve Ashley, but was eternally grateful that she'd been the one assigned to his sister's kidnapping.

Ten minutes into their meal, Danny began to cry and fuss. Cade jumped up to tend to the baby, realizing he needed to be changed. Afterward, he held his nephew in one arm as he quickly finished eating.

"Do you need me to take him?" Ashley offered.

"I'm good." He could only impose on her so much. "I hate to ask, but will there be another officer stationed outside tonight?"

"Yes, the chief agreed to extend that service after we found the shell casing. But I was thinking we should sleep in shifts anyway. Maybe four hours at a time. That way we can take care of the baby while keeping watch."

The idea of four uninterrupted hours of sleep was enticing. "Are you sure? Danny is my responsibility, not yours."

"It's a team effort," she said with a smile.

It was only a team effort because of her willingness to make it so. Something he doubted most officers would do. "I can take the first watch," he told her.

"You should sleep first, since I want to continue digging into Joe Jurgen's and Rafe Travon's backgrounds." Her smile dimmed. "Tomorrow, I plan to bring Elaine in for a formal interview."

"Sounds good." He wished he could watch Ashley interrogate the woman, but knew that was stretching it. "I'll hit the sack after I feed Danny one more time."

Sleep was amazingly healing. He and Ashley had taken turns with Danny and, by morning, Cade felt refreshed and eager to start the day. He was hopeful they'd find Melissa before nightfall. Ashley offered to make breakfast and watch Danny while he completed the morning chores.

An hour later he, Danny, Ozzy and Ashley were on the road in her K-9 SUV, heading back to Elk Valley. Normally, he didn't relish the idea of leaving the ranch, but he was keen to know if Elaine was involved.

"I assume you know Elaine's address?" Ashley asked.

"I do. She lives in a very small house a mile from the Chateau." He gave her directions on how to get there, and when Ashley turned into the driveway, he noticed the place was more dilapidated than he remembered.

Ashley voiced his thought. "Looks like the house and yard could use some maintenance."

"Yeah. I haven't been here in the six months since we broke up. Back then, she kept the place in good shape. Not sure what happened in the time since we've been split up." Was it possible Elaine had been more interested in living on his ranch than in him personally?

To be fair, she may have been more upset and depressed over their breakup than he'd given her credit for.

"Stay inside with Danny." Ashley shot him a stern look before emerging from the vehicle. After releasing her K-9 from the back, the pair headed to the front door. Ozzy sniffed the crumbling walkway with interest along the way.

There was no response to Ashley's knock. He watched as she and Ozzy walked around the property. Ashley peered in a few windows, but then returned to the SUV.

"We'll head to the Chateau next."

"Okay." They'd passed the beautiful hotel on their way, so it only took a few minutes to return. Once again, he was relegated to waiting while Ashley and Ozzy entered the hotel.

Less than five minutes later, though, they were back, Ashley's features appearing grim. She secured Ozzy in the rear of the SUV then slid in beside Cade. "Elaine called off sick today."

"Let's go back to the house, and knock again." He wasn't willing to give up.

"That's just it," Ashley said as she started the SUV. "She wasn't there. I looked for signs of someone being there, but the living room and bedrooms were empty."

"Empty." He stared blindly out the windshield as Ashley headed into town. If Elaine wasn't at home or at work—then where was she?

Ashley headed straight to the Elk Valley police station, determined to talk to the chief about obtaining a search warrant for Elaine's home. The bad news was that Ozzy hadn't alerted anywhere around the outside of the house, the way she'd hoped. If Elaine had used her brother to do the deed, she'd thought Ozzy would have alerted on his scent there. Without that, she wasn't sure an argument between the possible perp and the missing victim was enough.

"You and Danny need to come inside to wait." Ashley parked the SUV and killed the engine. "I don't know how long I'll be."

"That's fine. Take whatever you need to find Melissa." He didn't look frustrated at the delay, but she also got the sense Cade wasn't used to sitting around. She could relate.

She let Ozzy out and followed Cade and Danny inside. As father and nephew went over to sit in the chair along the side of the lobby, Ashley and Ozzy went to Nora's office.

"Hanson." Nora gave her a nod. "What do you have?"

"Elaine Jurgen isn't at home or at her job working the front desk at the Chateau." She quickly explained about the argument between Elaine and Melissa. "I'd like a search warrant to go through her house."

The words hadn't even left her mouth when Nora began shaking her head. "You need something that connects Jurgen to the kidnapping."

"I was afraid of that. Although, you have to admit, Elaine's being off work and away from home is suspicious."

Nora arched a brow. "Suspicious? She could have taken a spa day, or skipped out to see a friend."

"Yeah, okay. Fine." She sighed. "I'll keep digging. But so far, I've come up empty."

"Something will break soon." Her chief's tone was encouraging "But in the meantime, you need to touch base with Agent Rawlston."

"Will do, thanks." Ashley left the office, wondering what Chase wanted. She couldn't be in trouble if she hadn't been given an assignment in the murder investigation, could she?

She ran into Bennett Ford and his K-9, a beagle named Spike, on her way to the conference room.

"There you are," Bennett said. "Let's go."

"Go where?"

"Boss wants us to interview Evan Carr, Naomi's older brother to see if we can get anything out of him, and to verify his alibi for the timeframe of the murders."

Chase wanted her to participate in the interview? She tamped down the surge of elation. "I'm ready." Her gaze landed on Cade and Danny, making her wince. "I need two minutes to arrange for an officer to take Cade and Danny home."

"Hurry. Carr is expecting us."

Since she hadn't even known about the assignment, the minor delay was hardly her fault. But she wasn't going to let this opportunity pass, either. She briefed Cade on the update and promised to meet him back at the ranch when she was finished. Then she joined Bennett, a little surprised he was still in town. In their first meeting, she'd learned Bennett was a detective living in Colorado. Apparently, Chase had asked him to hang around for a few days. "Where are we going, exactly?"

"Evan Carr runs a professional recruiting business out of his home, two miles outside of Elk Valley. You and Ozzy can follow me."

"Okay." She wanted to inquire about Chase's change of

heart in assigning her to the interview, but decided it didn't matter. Maybe it was her obtaining Cowgirl for the team. Or maybe he valued her knowledge of their small community.

The trip to Evan's house didn't take long. The place was a beautiful log cabin, a stark contrast to Elaine's dilapidated home.

"I'll take the lead," Bennett said as they approached the front door. "But I want you to jump in with questions, too. If he gets feisty, you can play the role of good cop, soothing his fears."

"Understood," she agreed. "Although, to be honest, the times I've seen Evan around town, he's been nothing but polite and helpful."

"We'll see," Bennett said, his tone indicating he didn't believe it.

Evan Carr immediately opened the door at Bennett's knock. "Come in, both of you." He was tall and lean, but not muscular. Dressed in crisp tan slacks with a deep blue sweater pulled over a turtleneck, his blond hair perfectly styled, he had the look of a successful businessman. He was attractive enough, she supposed, but she secretly preferred Cade's rugged good looks.

"Thanks." Bennett led the way inside with Spike at his heel. Ozzy at her side, she closed the door behind them and followed as Evan walked to the kitchen. The place was immaculately clean, making her wonder if he'd ever cooked a meal there.

"Can I get you anything? Coffee, water, tea?" Evan looked at them expectantly. His gaze dropped to their dogs for a moment before returning to them. She was curious about the flash of compassion in his eyes.

"No thanks," Bennett said.

"I'm fine, too." She gestured to their K-9s. "You don't mind us having the dogs here, do you?"

"Not at all. I love dogs." His expression turned pained. "I recently lost my female chocolate Lab, Kiko."

"Oh, I'm sorry to hear that." Ashley couldn't imagine losing Ozzy.

Evan gave a solemn nod. "Thanks."

Bennett cleared his throat, no doubt trying to get the interview back on track. "I appreciate your willingness to talk with us, Evan."

"Of course, anything to help bring justice for the families of those poor victims." Evan took a seat across the table from them. "What would you like to know?"

"Do you think it's possible your sister was so upset over being humiliated by the YRC victims at the semiformal dance ten years ago that she sought revenge and killed them?" Bennett's blunt question caught Ashley off guard.

Evan, too. His eyes rounded in surprise. "Naomi? Killing anyone? That's absurd!" His shock seemed real. "Naomi is a sweetheart without a mean or spiteful bone in her body. What happened that night was hurtful, and I know she cried her eyes out afterward. And, yes, those guys should have been ashamed of their cruel actions, but to take the next step of seeking revenge and shooting them in cold blood?" He shook his head. "No way. That's impossible."

"Naomi is several years younger than you, right?" Bennett pressed on. "I was under the impression you weren't that close, so how do you know for sure?"

"She is four years younger, yes, and while we may not be that close, we're not estranged, either. We always get together on holidays." Evan shot them incredulous looks. "You can't seriously consider her a suspect. She's a widow and eight months pregnant. It's all she can do to support herself by running her deceased husband's tour company out in Denver. I saw her at Ted's funeral six months ago. She was wrecked over losing him."

"I can certainly understand how difficult that must have been for her," Ashley said, playing her role of peacemaker. She was sad to hear that her former high school friend was a widow and eight months pregnant. "More so because she's expecting. It's good that she has you to lean on during this terrible time."

Evan seemed somewhat mollified. "I've been trying to do my part in supporting her through this… I'm planning to make the trip out to Denver when she has the baby."

"That will be wonderful for both of you." Ashley smiled encouragingly. "How did her husband die?"

"Ted was out scoping the mountains for new hiking trails. He wanted something new to offer their clients, something the other tour companies wouldn't have, but he must have taken a misstep as he was found at the bottom of a ravine." Evan's eyes darkened. "It's awful that he died so young."

"Yes, it certainly is," Ashley murmured. She glanced at Bennett, expecting him to take over the interview, but he gave her a slight nod, indicating she should keep going. "Evan, I know this might be upsetting, but I need to ask where you were the night Seth Jenkins, Brad Kingsley and Aaron Anderson were murdered."

"I'm not upset. I already gave my alibi to the detectives when I spoke to them ten years ago." Evan spread his hands wide. "I have nothing to hide. I was with my girlfriend at the time, Paulina Potter. We were together all night."

She remembered reading that in the reports Chase had submitted to the team prior to their first meeting. She held Evan's gaze. "And you have no idea who could have killed those three men? Or the two recent victims?"

"None whatsoever." He shook his head slowly, his expression full of distress. "I knew all those guys in the Young Rancher's Club, not that we were close friends or anything, but this town isn't that big. To lose three young men in one night was terrible. I know you're asking about this because of the two new murders across the Rockies, and I am appalled that this brazen killer has struck again." He stared at her with concern. "I just hope he stays far away from Elk Valley and has left Denver, where my sister lives."

"We all do," she assured him, trying to come up with another question. She glanced at Bennett again, but he simply shrugged. She removed a business card from her pocket and slid it across the table. "Thanks again for your cooperation, Evan. If you think of anything else that would help us, please call me."

"I promise I will." Evan set the card aside as he rose to his feet to escort them back to the front door. She noticed he gave the dogs one last, longing glance before closing the door behind them.

Outside, Bennett didn't say anything until they were near their respective vehicles. "What did you think?" Bennett asked.

"He seemed sincere," she said. "Although we obviously still need to follow up with Pauline Potter on his alibi."

"Yeah." Bennett turned to look at the house. "His business is obviously successful. Seems odd to me that he'd risk everything to kill these guys. To avenge his sister? Sounds like a stretch. But anything is possible."

"I agree." She opened the back of her SUV and gestured for Ozzy to jump up. "Should we head to the station to update the boss?"

"I'll take care of it. I know you're working the kidnapping case, too." Bennett gave her a nod. "Evan really connected with you, Ashley. Good work."

His praise was nice, although she would have rather Chase impressed with her work. As she drove back through town, then out onto the highway toward the McNeal Four

Ranch, she was secretly pleased to have been included in the interview.

She'd prove herself worthy of being included on the task force yet.

On the heels of that thought came the memory of Cade's warm and strong embrace last night. Crossing the line with a victim was the quickest way to lose her boss's respect.

No more, she silently chided. Cade was off limits. Adorable Danny, too. If there was anything she'd learned from her father, it was that she needed to stay focused on her career.

NINE

Officer Volt sat in Cade's kitchen, sipping coffee. Cade didn't like having the guy there, he missed Ashley's reassuring presence. Oh, he trusted this cop could protect Danny. The problem was that he felt more comfortable asking Ashley to help with caring for his nephew. Because she was a woman? The thought made him wince.

When his phone rang, he quickly grabbed it. Relief washed over him upon seeing Ashley's number on the screen. "Ashley? Everything okay?"

"Yes, of course." Was there a sense of impatience in her tone? As if she didn't like his questioning her ability? "I'm on my way to the ranch."

"Great. I'll let Officer Volt know." Hearing his name, the officer quirked a brow. "See you soon."

"Yep." Ashley disconnected from the call.

"You heard?" he asked. Officer Volt didn't say anything, but continued to sip his coffee.

Danny squirmed and began to cry. Cade quickly lifted the baby from his seat and carried him down the hall to the nursery to change him.

He liked when Danny was awake and looking up at him. He hadn't taken the time to read all the baby books Melissa had gotten, so he wasn't sure how long it would be until his nephew began to smile or track to a voice.

Did his nephew miss his mother?

His hope for a quick resolution to Melissa's kidnapping

was fading fast. What if they didn't find her? What if the kidnapper had hurt her? Or worse? He couldn't imagine how he'd cope with raising Danny without his mother.

Shying away from those thoughts, he did his best to stay positive. He needed to have faith in God, and in Ashley, and the rest of the Elk Valley police department.

"We're going to be fine, right, big guy?" He smiled when his nephew accidently hit himself in the face. An expert at changing diapers, Cade finished the job and lifted Danny into his arms. The baby curled against him in a simple act of faith and trust.

Returning to the kitchen, Cade stared out at the barn. He desperately needed to get out there to care for his horses. The few chores he'd been able to accomplish weren't enough. Not by a long shot.

Volt stood and stretched his muscles. "Hanson will be here in five minutes. I'm heading out to the squad car. You and the kid should stay inside."

"Fine." Cade didn't bother to object. Since Danny was still awake, he made a bottle, anticipating he'd soon announce his desire to eat. Sure enough, Danny began making squeaking noises then let out a full-blown wail.

"I'm coming, big guy." He shook the bottle to dissolve the powdered formula in the warm water then sat to feed the boy. Danny's dark eyes clung to his, melting his heart.

Ten minutes later, Ashley and Ozzy arrived. She looked satisfied, as if the interview had gone well.

"Did you get some good information?" he asked.

She nodded but did not elaborate. "I'm sure you'd like to head out to the barn."

"Yes, I really need to tend to the horses." He glanced down at Danny. "As soon as he's finished here."

She bent to pat Ozzy's head. "I plan to focus my investigation on both Joe Jurgen and Rafe Travon. It's possible Elaine hired one of them to kidnap Melissa."

"Anything is possible. No sign of Elaine yet?"

"Nope. Nora agreed to issue a BOLO on her as a person of interest but we couldn't get a search warrant." She shrugged. "Hopefully, we'll have a chance to interview her very soon."

He'd prefer Elaine be tossed in jail, but he supposed they needed more evidence against her first. Maybe tracking Rafe Travon and Joe Jurgen would provide whatever Ashley needed to accomplish that task.

Danny's eyes closed as sleepiness took over. Cade set the bottle aside then shifted the baby so that he could rest upright against his shoulder, remembering at the last minute to use a rag to protect his shirt.

After the baby emitted a soft burp, he stood and set him in the infant seat. Glancing at the clock, he noted the morning was more than half over.

"I'm heading to the barn." He gestured at Ashley's computer. "I hope you find something good while I'm gone. And if you get hungry, help yourself to whatever is in the fridge."

"Thanks." She smiled. "I was thinking we could have grilled cheese sandwiches for lunch."

"You don't have to cook for me." He felt obligated to protest. "I can make them when I'm finished."

Her brow furrowed. "It's no problem. I don't mind."

And that was exactly why he liked her so much. "Thanks. I am very grateful for everything you're doing for me and Danny."

"It's not like I don't have to eat, too." She didn't meet his gaze but stayed focused on the computer.

Taking that as a sign to get moving, he shrugged into his coat, set his Stetson on his head, and reached for the rifle.

He strode out to the barn, sweeping his scrutiny around the area, searching for any indication of trouble. Reassured, he entered the building and went to work.

As he mucked stalls and threw out fresh hay, he heard a thumping followed by a huffing sound coming from Spark's stall. The gelding was a thoroughbred and his best mountain horse. A chill snaked down Cade's spine when Spark sent a sharp kick against the stall. That wasn't usual.

Someone was in the barn! He emerged from the empty stall he'd been cleaning to grab the rifle. A flash of movement had him turning to lift his arm, instinctively deflecting the blow from a rake. A man wearing a ski mask loomed beside him.

Melissa's kidnapper!

Anger burned in his belly. Cade saw the rake in the guy's hand. He darted forward, grabbing it with adrenaline-fueled strength.

The assailant surprised him by letting go then drawing his gun. Since he didn't have his rifle in hand, all Cade could do was to drop and roll into the empty stall, awkwardly bringing the rake with him.

Gunfire echoed, spooking his horses. Loud whinnies and the thumping of hooves expressed their discontent. Cade jumped to his feet and peered around the edge of the stall.

A flash of movement caught his eye. A dark shadow disappearing down the long hall between the two rows of stalls.

He was going to escape!

Cade charged after him, doing his best to ignore the sound of panic from his frightened horses.

He could not let this guy get away!

A gunshot!

Ashley used her radio to notify the dispatcher, even as

she pulled her weapon from its holster. "This is Unit 7. Gunfire at the McNeal Four Ranch. Send backup!"

She stepped toward the door then glanced at Danny. She couldn't leave him! Thinking fast, she remembered the baby harness Cade had used. She found the device, managed to strap it on, then carefully tucked Danny into the front so he was snuggled against her.

She zipped her jacket as far as it would go, adding more reinforcement. When she was convinced Danny was secure, she glanced at her dog. "Come, Ozzy."

Her K-9 partner kept pace with her as she lightly ran to the barn, holding her free hand securely over Danny. Reaching the door, she paused to take a breath.

Easing it open a crack, she peered inside.

The barn was long and narrow, with stalls on both sides. The horses thumped and neighed, clearly upset by the gunfire. When she didn't see anyone, she pushed the door open and stepped in.

On the other side of the barn, Ashley could see that the opposite door was wide open. Yet that didn't mean the gunman wasn't inside, waiting for her. She wouldn't risk Danny or her K-9 partner, so she eased forward, carefully clearing one stall and then the other as she made her way down the center aisle.

"Cade? Are you in here?"

No response other than the restless sounds of the horses. Her heart thudded painfully against her ribs. Had the intruder wounded Cade? Had he been kidnapped, too?

Dear Lord, protect him!

She was only halfway down the main aisle when she saw Cade coming through the doorway up ahead. "Ashley? What are you doing here? Where's Danny?"

"I have him." A wave of relief hit hard, but she continued painstakingly clearing each stall in case there had been more than one shooter.

Ozzy sniffed each space with interest, too. Her K-9 hadn't spent much time around horses, and she didn't doubt he was already embedding each new scent in his amazing memory. Labs like Ozzy could store up to one hundred million unique scents in their brains. This ability made him an incredible tracker.

"I chased the guy toward the woods, but lost him." Cade's voice was laden with disgust. "I wanted to keep going, but knew Ozzy had better skills to find him."

"He does." She finished the last stall, stopping beside him. Despite her determination to keep her distance, she hated knowing how close Cade had been to being struck by a bullet. "You aren't hit?"

"No." He scowled. "I wish I could have hit him, though. He spooked the horses."

And nearly killed Cade. She swallowed hard. "I heard." She rested her hand on Danny's back. "Backup is on the way. I'll need you to take the baby, so I can take Ozzy out to track this guy."

"Sure." Cade took Danny so she could remove the dog's harness. Then he gestured to the rake lying on the ground. "He tried to club me on the head with the rake, Ozzy might be able to get a scent from the handle. Although I grabbed it from his hands, so my scent is on it, too."

"Ozzy is good, he'll follow the right scent trail. Even if the assailant wore gloves, his scent would still cling to the material." She was confident in her K-9's ability. She bent to make sure Ozzy's bullet-resistant vest was secure.

"Ready to work, Oz?" She smiled when the K-9 wagged his tail in agreement.

"Be careful, Ashley. This guy has a gun and isn't afraid to use it."

"Same goes for me, too." She'd never been in a position to use deadly force, but would not hesitate to do what was necessary to protect innocent lives.

The sound of a police siren reached her ears. Through the barn door, she could see two vehicles with lights flashing coming down the ranch driveway. She was anxious for Ozzy to hit the trail; every second that passed grated on her nerves.

She led Ozzy outside to meet her backup. To her surprise, she recognized Bennett behind the wheel of the SUV. He must have still been talking to Chase about their interview with Evan Carr, when her request for assistance had gone through. In the squad behind him, she recognized Officer Volt.

Bennett emerged from the vehicle first. "Hanson." He greeted her with a curt nod. "You and Ozzy shouldn't track this guy alone. Spike and I will go with you."

"Great." She was touched by his offer. She'd initially thought the task force members felt sorry for her, but maybe she'd been wrong. It seemed as if Bennett and Meadow were treating her as a productive member of the team. "There's a rake inside the barn to use as a scent source. According to Cade, the guy tried to hit him then fired his gun and ran off, disappearing into the woods." She glanced at Bennett's beagle, Spike. He was trained to find narcotics, but she knew he was capable of tracking people, too, if necessary. "I'll take the lead with Ozzy, if that's okay?"

"Absolutely. We'll be right behind you," Bennett said.

She entered the barn and walked to the rake. Leaving it on the ground, she pointed at it. "Rake, Ozzy. This is Rake."

The K-9 sniffed all along the rake's handle, taking his time to fill his senses. She glanced over to where Cade had joined them, Danny tucked into the harness on his chest.

"Ozzy? This is Cade." She put her hand on Cade's forearm. "Cade."

Ozzy's came over to sniff him, tail wagging with excitement, indicating his approval of Cade.

She walked toward the open doorway on the opposite side of the barn from where they'd entered. "Seek! Seek Rake!"

All signs of playfulness disappeared as Ozzy immediately lowered his nose to the ground then lifted his snout to the air. She heard Bennett talking to Spike behind her, but stayed focused on her dog. Ozzy trotted through the open barn doorway. She kept him off leash, knowing it wouldn't be easy for him to follow the scent through the woods with being tethered to her. Yet she also feared for his safety. Tracking this guy was a necessary risk, so she forced herself to let it go.

"Seek Rake," she repeated. Not that Ozzy needed much encouragement. He followed the invisible scent trail across the open field, zigzagging between patches of snow.

Ashley hurried to keep up with him, scanning the woods for signs of a threat. She wanted to find this guy, but the possibility he was hiding in the woods with a gun trained on her and Ozzy nagged at her. She held her service weapon, ready to protect her partner.

Focusing on the possible threat, she continued following Ozzy as he entered the woods. They'd only gone about twenty yards in before Ozzy turned to the left. He stayed on that scent trail for a while, moving parallel to the pasture below.

There wasn't a doubt in her mind that her K-9 was on the scent of the assailant. Cade hadn't followed the perp this far, and Ozzy didn't hesitate as he darted between trees. Every so often, she caught the hint of a heel print in the snow, similar to the one Ozzy had found in the Elk Valley Park parking lot, but didn't take the time to mark them now.

Not if there was the chance Ozzy would lead her straight to the gunman.

She heard Bennett and Spike working several yards behind her, but didn't slow her pace. Or rather, Ozzy's pace. The K-9 moved swiftly, forcing her to jog to keep up.

The dense trees surrounding them eased her fear that the gunman was hiding nearby, intending to shoot. Logically, it made sense for him to get off the ranch rather than to wait around for them.

But she wasn't taking any chances. Not with her partner's life. Or Cade's and Danny's, either.

Soon, Ozzy was heading back down the slope. Her heart sinking, she trailed after him. When the Lab led her straight to a dirt road, she groaned out loud.

Ozzy sniffed intently along the ground for several long moments before turning to sit. He stared up at her, his dark eyes locked on hers.

"Good boy, Oz!" She generously praised him, reaching for the rope toy in her vest pouch. "Good boy!"

She tossed the rope toy away from the dirt road and then turned her attention to the rutted earth. There were no clear tire tracks, the ground having been frozen, then thawing briefly at a brief stint of warm weather, before freezing again. There was a small dark spot in the ground. She knelt and sniffed. Yep, it was oil.

Looking for a vehicle that leaked oil wasn't much help. The heel prints she'd passed were probably the best evidence, if they could match the tread to the heel print found the night of Melissa's kidnapping.

It wasn't enough. A wave of frustration hit hard. They needed more!

"Is this the end of the trail?" Bennett's voice interrupted her thoughts.

"Yes. There's a small oil spot here. It's still wet so likely left by the perp's vehicle." She smiled as Ozzy nudged her leg with his nose, chew toy in his mouth. She took the rope and tossed it again. Ozzy bounded after it. "Did you take note of the heel prints?"

"I did. I marked the two I found with a flag." Bennett grinned as Ozzy galloped toward them. "Nice work following the scent trail."

"Yeah. For all the good it did." She tried not to sound as discouraged as she felt.

"Seems this perp is familiar with the McNeal Four Ranch," Bennett said. "How else would he know about this dirt road? It's in the middle of nowhere."

She pursed her lips. "You think he may have worked the ranch at some point?"

"Why not?" Bennett shrugged. "I suppose it's possible he spent some time casing the place, but you'd think McNeal would have noticed."

"True. I'll ask Cade to provide a list of ranch hands he's had working for him over the past few years." Another list, more hours of digging into people's backgrounds. She was very familiar with the tedium of paperwork, but knowing Melissa was out there, being held against her will, made it difficult to have the patience she needed.

"Let's head back," Bennett suggested.

She nodded and called Ozzy over. Rather than go up into the woods, they took a direct route to the ranch house. When they arrived, Cade looked at her with frank hope in his eyes. Seeing her dejected expression caused the light to drain from his eyes.

"He's gone."

"Yes." She shook her head helplessly. "Ozzy followed

the scent trail through the woods and down to a dirt road. He must have left a vehicle there, using it to escape."

Cade turned away, raking his hand over his disheveled hair. She could feel the frustration and sorrow radiating off him.

The need to wrap her arms around him was strong, but she forced herself to stay back.

Maintaining a professional distance from Cade and Danny was proving to be as difficult as finding Melissa.

And it wasn't good that she was failing at both tasks.

TEN

If only he'd grabbed him! Cade ground his molars together, battling frustration. He shouldn't have been caught off guard. Why hadn't he expected the guy to show up again? Sure, he'd pulled the rake from the assailant's hands, but hadn't yanked hard enough to throw him off balance.

Now the guy had escaped and they were no closer to finding Melissa.

Ozzy's wet nose nudged his hand, bringing a reluctant smile. He bent to scratch the black Lab behind the ears. There was nothing better than the pure love from a dog. Yeah, it was time to get another collie. As soon as they found Melissa and reunited her with Danny.

"Cade, is there anything you can tell me about the gunman?"

Ashley's question had him turning toward her. The other K-9 cop, Detective Bennett, had gone with the officer who'd responded as backup, to evaluate the evidence they'd found along the trail. Gathering his thoughts, he nodded. "The horses were restless, giving me a hint that something was wrong. But the masked man was already bringing the rake down on my head before I realized what was going on. I managed to block the blow and wrench the rake from his grip."

"How tall was he?"

He frowned, doing his best to bring those blurred moments into sharp focus. "Shorter than me. I'm six feet, two inches tall, so maybe five-ten or five-eleven."

"Great, what about his build?"

"Not as muscular as I'd expected. I was able to grab the rake easily enough. But then he pulled a gun and began shooting." It burned to know his rifle had been propped in the corner of the tack room, essentially useless. "I ducked into the stall to avoid being hit. The horses panicked at the gunfire, making all kinds of noise. It took me a minute to figure out he was using the chaos to get away. That's when I took off after him."

Ashley's brow creased with concern. "That was risky, Cade. He was armed and you weren't."

"Tell me about it." He wished he owned a handgun, but didn't. "I had my rifle propped in the corner of the tack room, but I didn't think of grabbing it. As it turned out, the guy was a bad shot, didn't come close to hitting me."

"That's interesting, because most guys out here are decent shots."

"Yeah." If Elaine was responsible, had she given orders not to kill him? At this point, he didn't know what to think.

"What is it?" Ashley asked.

"Nothing." He gave himself a mental shake. "I wish there was more I could tell you about this guy, but I had to hide when he started shooting."

She rested her hand on his forearm. "You need to be careful, Cade. Danny needs you."

"I know." He glanced toward the baby, sitting in his infant seat on the table. "But Danny needs his mother, too."

"We'll find her." Ashley lightly squeezed his arm and he reached over to cover her hand with his. The warmth from her skin helped ease his self-disgust over failing to get this guy.

Ashley slipped her hand from his and leaned down to

pet Ozzy. Her cheeks were pink, likely from the way she'd been running around outside in the cold. "I need a list of your ranch hands, going back at least two years ago."

His eyebrow levered up. "Why?"

"This perp seems familiar with your ranch, Cade." She straightened to face him. "How else did he know about the rutted dirt road? You can't see it from the house."

"That road is used by me and Roger's crew, too." At her blank look, he clarified. "Roger Ward, of the Rocking W Ranch. His land butts up against mine."

"I see. That means we'll need a list of his ranch hands, as well."

"He has a ranch foreman, Earl Sloan, who works year-round." Cade had been the foreman here when his father was alive. After his death, it was all he could do to keep the ranch running in the black while raising his younger sister. There hadn't been money to hire another foreman. "Aside from Earl, Roger hires on temporary help as needed, the way I do. It isn't that unusual for us to share ranch hands back and forth, either."

"Earl Sloan." Ashley pulled a small notebook from her pocket and jotted the name down. "I need to talk to Earl and Roger."

"About their ranch hands?" He frowned. "You don't think they're involved in Melissa's kidnapping, do you? They have no reason to get rid of her or Danny."

"I'm keeping an open mind. But that brings up another idea. Who gets first crack at buying your ranch if you decide to sell?"

Ashley's question was like a sucker punch to the gut. Was this really about the McNeal Four Ranch? No, that couldn't be right. He managed to keep his emotions under control. "Roger does. But that would mean he'd need to get a loan and come up with some additional cash. The past two years have not been as good as we'd hoped. Besides, Roger would never stoop so low. He and my dad were friends. We've always helped each other out as needed."

"I know this is difficult, Cade." Her blue eyes held his. "But we need to investigate any and all possibilities."

"Even lifelong friends." He didn't hide the bitterness in his tone. The more he thought about the possibility of someone getting the ranch as motive for the kidnapping, the less he believed it. If that was the case, he'd have been the target, not Melissa and Danny. With him out of the way, his sister would have been forced into selling the place. Since Roger had first dips on the property it would make more sense for him or anyone interested in the ranch to hurt Cade, not Melissa.

He shook his head, irritated all over again. "You're barking up the wrong tree, Ashley. I'm the one that would have been targeted if the intent was to grab the ranch. Go ahead and talk to Roger and Earl, especially about the ranch hands, but do it fast so that you can get back on track to find the real kidnapper."

"I will." Ashley took his flash of anger in stride. "Is there anything else you can remember from the altercation in the barn?"

He thought back to those moments then shook his head. "No. It sounds cliché, but it all happened so fast."

"That's totally understandable. I'd still like that list of ranch hands."

"I'll get it now." He'd moved his office into the master bedroom to make more room in the living space for Danny's baby swing. Taking Danny's carrier with him, unwilling to let the baby out of his sight, he headed down the hall. He set Danny's infant seat on the bed.

Ashley and Ozzy hovered in the doorway as he booted

up the computer. He printed off a report that included the names of his temporary help over the past three years.

It wasn't a super-long list, twelve names total. When the paper spit out of the printer, he added the numbers for Earl and Roger before handing it to Ashley. "Here you go."

"Thank you." She scanned the list, no doubt looking for familiar names. Living in downtown Elk Valley, she may be more familiar with the younger guys than he realized. "I see Mike Stucky is on the list."

"You know Mike?"

She shrugged. "I told you about my former boyfriend. Mike and I dated last summer."

The stab of jealousy surprised him. Of course, guys would be interested in dating Ashley. She was beautiful, sweet and fun. It just never occurred to him that she'd have dated one of his ranch hands.

One of his much younger ranch hands. He remembered Mike always bragging about his female conquests. It stung to know Ashley was one of them. And it also made him angry at how badly the cowboy had treated her.

"I'm sorry." His belated response had her looking up at him in surprise.

"For what? Oh, you mean because of the way Mike cheated on me?" She wrinkled her nose. "It doesn't matter. He was only interested in having a good time. Not really my type."

Who is your type? He managed to hold back from voicing the question out loud.

Whomever Ashley dated wasn't any of his business. He shouldn't even be thinking about her on a personal level. Not when his sister was still suffering at the hands of her kidnapper. She could be injured, or worse, dead.

His gaze landed on Danny's peaceful sleeping face. His

heart squeezed painfully and he silently promised he would not rest until he knew for sure one way or the other.

Keeping her distance from Cade wasn't easy. Ashley stared blindly at the list of names for a few minutes, until the urge to hug him passed.

"Can you stay for a while yet?" Cade asked. "I didn't get to finish caring for the horses."

She didn't like the idea of him heading out to the barn again, but he couldn't just leave the livestock to fend for themselves. She glanced at Bennett's text, informing her he was heading to the precinct and that Officer Gerund was, too. "Sure, that's fine," she told Cade. "I'll start looking for connections between these ranch hands and Elaine Jurgen." She hesitated then added, "When do you want to eat lunch?"

The corner of his mouth quirked. "Now that you mention it, I could eat."

"I'll start the grilled cheese." As she turned to head into the kitchen, her phone rang. Surprised to see her father's name, she quickly answered. "Hey, Dad."

"Ashley, I wanted to let you know Cowgirl will be brought to the police station at nine o'clock tomorrow morning."

"Thanks, Dad." She had to give him credit for working fast. "I know the victims' families will appreciate having Cowgirl to help them cope with their loss."

"I agree." Her dad's attitude surprised her. He wasn't normally the touchy-feely type. "You haven't said much about the task force's progress."

"Bennett Ford and I conducted an interview earlier today and I know others are doing their assigned tasks, too. We're all determined to get this killer."

"Good to know." His response made her wonder if he'd already gotten an update from Chase.

"Listen, Dad, I'm in the middle of a few things, and I need to follow up with Liana Lightfoot, our dog trainer, about Cowgirl's impending arrival. I'll talk to you later, okay?"

"Sure thing." Her father disconnected.

She quickly called Liana, leaving Cade with the task of making lunch despite her offer to help. It was probably better that she had to make a few calls. Difficult enough to remain professional when she wasn't working alongside Cade in the cozy intimacy of the kitchen.

After she filled Liana in on Cowgirl's arrival, she made one more call to her chief. "I have a list of ranch hands from Cade McNeal. I could use some help from Isla in getting background checks done on these guys."

"What makes you suspect one of them of being involved?" Nora asked.

She summarized the attack against Cade and how Ozzy had tracked the perp to a rutted dirt road located between the McNeal Four and Rocking W ranches. "It's just a thought, one I don't want to overlook. I'm going to talk to both the owner and foreman of the Rocking W, too."

"Okay. Send me the names and I'll ask Isla to run them. She should have something by the end of the day, or tomorrow at the latest."

"Thanks." She ended the call and used her phone to take a picture of the list of ranch hands. Once she'd sent it to the chief, she glanced down at Ozzy. "I need to take Oz outside. I'll be back soon."

Cade shot a quick look over his shoulder. "No problem. These will be done shortly, though."

She nodded and slipped outside. The cold March air hit hard and she huddled in her coat as she told Ozzy to get busy.

Looking around the ranch, she wondered where the

property lines were located. Could the ranch itself be the reason for the kidnapping? It was a beautiful piece of property and one that spanned many acres.

Her thoughts returned to Elaine Jurgen, who'd called in sick yet wasn't at home. Was she off somewhere meeting with the thug she'd hired to kidnap Melissa and Cade? One of the names on Cade's list? Or had she simply taken a spa day, as Nora had suggested?

The endless possibilities of who was responsible for kidnapping Melissa weighed heavily on Ashley's shoulders. She didn't want to fail Cade and Danny.

When she and Ozzy returned to the kitchen, Cade was sliding golden brown grilled cheese sandwiches on two plates. She took a moment to wash up before joining him at the table. Danny was still sleeping in his infant seat.

Cade bowed his head. "Dear Lord Jesus, we thank You for this food before us. We ask that You please keep Melissa safe and provide the police with the strength, courage and knowledge they need to bring her home. Amen."

"Amen." The way Cade prayed for his sister was humbling. It made Ashley wonder if anyone would have done that for her if she'd disappeared.

"You mentioned looking at Elaine's social media. Have you found anything helpful?"

His question brought her back to the issue at hand. "Not yet, but I've barely scratched the surface. Having the names of your ranch hands will help."

He nodded. "I don't use social media, there's no time in my life for that stuff, so I don't know that much about it."

"I often use social media sites to find information on perps, so I'll take care of it." She hoped there would be time to do that before Danny woke up again.

"You must think I'm old fashioned," Cade muttered.

"What?" She was surprised by his comment. "No, why

would I? You have much more important things to do with your time. I only have a site so I can look at other people's profiles. Most cops don't want their personal lives plastered out there for everyone to see."

"Oh, that makes sense."

Danny woke, squirming and crying. Cade jumped up to care for the baby. She finished her sandwich and carried her dishes to the sink, filling it with hot soapy water. Cade changed the baby then fed him, eating the last of his second sandwich with one hand.

She finished the dishes and then opened the computer. Cade edged closer, watching over her shoulder. Since Elaine had been his fiancée, Ashley didn't see the harm in allowing him to see who Elaine was connected with online.

"Hey, who is that guy?" Cade leaned closer, the hint of aftershave mingled with straw and horses teased her senses. "Jeremy Weller? I haven't heard that name before."

"Let's find out." She navigated the site, pulling up a profile photo of Weller. "Says here he's the general manager at the Elk Valley Chateau."

"He looks short and husky in that picture." Cade frowned. "No way is he the assailant."

"I agree." Weller didn't fit the profile at all. She went back to Elaine's information and continued checking the names of the woman's friends. She stiffened when she saw Melissa's name. She glanced at him. "Your sister is listed as her friend. I looked at Melissa's social media pages early on, but I didn't notice this connection."

Cade's green eyes darkened. "I'm sure that was before Elaine confronted her at the Rusty Spoke."

"Probably." She clicked to get more information from Melissa's social media page. As she'd noted before, there hadn't been any posts for well over nine months. Probably around the time she'd discovered she was pregnant with

Danny. "Melissa hasn't been active on her various social media profiles."

"How many friends does she have?" Cade appeared interested on what his sister was up to.

"Not that many." She clicked on them. "Most of them are employees from the Rusty Spoke." She paused when she saw the name Mike Stucky. Her former boyfriend, a local cowboy. "Looks like Melissa knew Mike, too."

"You need to check that guy out," Cade said in a flat tone. "I don't like the connection."

"What connection?" She turned in her seat to face him head-on. "People accept friend requests without thinking too much about them. Just because Melissa was friends with Mike on social media, or in person, doesn't mean he kidnapped her. What would be his motive?"

"Well, if you put it like that..." He sighed.

She shook her head, offering a wry grin. "I hate to say this, but there's probably a lot your sister did that you were oblivious to."

"I know. Danny is proof of that." He glanced at the infant then quickly added, "I wouldn't change anything, though. Babies are a blessing from God and I know Melissa loves her son. She's a good mother to him."

"I'm sure she is." Ashley turned her attention back to the computer screen. Having Cade hovering over her shoulder was unnerving. She continued going through Melissa's small list of friends, but didn't see any other familiar names.

Not even Vincent's.

Assuming Melissa had deleted him, maybe even blocked him, she moved on to review Elaine's page. She stumbled across Mike Stucky's name, along with Stuart Berg's.

Stuart's name had also been on Cade's list of ranch hands. She put a star next to his name on her list then added a star to Mike's name, too.

Ashley knew Mike was a handsome guy. After all, women had practically thrown themselves at him, or so he'd claimed when she'd caught him kissing another girl at the Rusty Spoke. Mike was all charm and no substance. She had little doubt he was still playing the field and enjoying every moment.

When she clicked on Stuart's profile picture, a handsome blond man grinned back at her. Not unlike Mike's profile picture. Both guys wore Western-styled shirts and cowboy hats.

Neither of them seemed to possess the innate confidence and self-assurance of Cade McNeal, though.

"Is that Stu?" Cade asked, interrupting her thoughts. "He was one of my better ranch hands."

"And one of Elaine's friends via social media." She stared at the picture of the smiling cowboy for a long moment. Then she toggled back to see Mike's profile picture. One she was very familiar with. Mike had light brown hair, but the rakish smile was just like Stuart's.

Two young men who knew the layout of the McNeal Four Ranch and were associated with Elaine on a personal level. Well, on a somewhat personal level. Social media could be deceiving. Some people added friends simply because they were associated with others.

Yet the connection was staring at her from the screen.

A coincidence?

She didn't believe in such.

They had a lot of suspects to consider, but she decided these two guys needed to be moved to the top of the list.

ELEVEN

Cade headed back out to the barn, rifle in hand. Deciding he needed to think like a cop, he went through the entire building to make sure there were no surprises. The horses were calmer now. Spark, his favorite thoroughbred, nuzzled his hand with a velvet nose, long black tail swishing from side to side.

Satisfied, he slung the rifle strap over his shoulder and went back to work. The rifle felt ungainly on his back, but he did his best to ignore it. No more leaving it in the tack room, that was for sure.

Knowing his young ranch hands may have played a part in Melissa's kidnapping had him seething with anger. Granted, he knew Ashley was right about how they shouldn't jump to conclusions, but the way the road between his ranch and Roger's spread had been used by the gunman to escape had him leaning toward their involvement.

Normally, he loved the routine of ranch chores, but right now, being forced to be here gnawed at him. He wanted to do something, anything, to help Ashley find his sister. It was horrible to imagine what Melissa might be suffering at the kidnapper's hands.

His brief tussle with the gunman replayed over and over in his mind.

When he nearly got kicked by Amber, his mare, he forced himself to concentrate on caring for the animals.

Once the stalls were clean, he led the horses out to the

pasture. He couldn't keep them cooped up forever. They needed to run and graze.

When he had all five horses in the pasture, he stood at the fence for a moment, watching them. He'd planned to breed Amber next month with Roger's stallion, Zeus. Now he couldn't seem to bring himself to think about the spring tasks ahead of him. Not until Melissa was home, safe and sound.

Turning away, he strode back to the ranch house. He'd left Danny with Ashley long enough. Her willingness to help him care for his nephew was a blessing, but he didn't want to take advantage of her kindness.

When he entered the kitchen, Ozzy came running over to greet him, tail wagging. He bent to pet the dog, frowning when he saw Ashley standing at the stove. The enticing scent of ground beef wafted toward him. "What are you doing?"

"Oh, hi." She tossed him a smile over her shoulder. "I poked around to find something basic I could make for dinner. Figured you wouldn't mind if I made tacos."

"You didn't have to do that." Not only was she caring for Danny, but she was taking care of him, too.

"I have to eat, too, right?" Her teasing tone brought a smile to his face. "Oz, leave him alone. You're acting like he was gone for days instead of hours."

"I don't mind. And you're already going above and beyond the call of duty." He should have come in earlier, but he'd taken advantage of the time he'd needed to get the work done.

"It's not a problem."

He removed his rifle, shrugged out of his coat and hung his Stetson on a peg before crossing to the sink to wash up. "I don't deserve you."

His voice came out low and husky, vibrating with emotion. Maybe the events of the day had gotten to him. That and her sweet kindness.

"Hey, anyone else would do the same." She waved off his gratitude.

That wasn't true, and being here earlier with Officer Volt was proof of that. Cade cleared his throat and tried to lighten the tone as he stepped back. "Did Danny behave for you?"

"He's a baby, how bad can he be?" She quirked an eyebrow. "Just wait until he's two and his favorite word is no."

Despite everything that had transpired, he chuckled at the image of Danny running around yelling no at the top of his lungs. "I can hardly wait." A sudden thought occurred to him. "Do you have siblings?"

"Me? No." Her expression turned wry. "My parents' marriage didn't survive one kid, much less two or three. My mom is remarried now and living in Arizona. She seems happy."

"I'm sorry to hear about the divorce." His parents had been married for over thirty years when they'd died. He should have known that his feelings for Elaine were nothing like the love that had shone from his father's eyes when he was with his mother. And vice versa. "Must have been tough."

"Not as much as you'd think." She shrugged, her expression nonchalant. "My dad traveled for work, so he wasn't home much when they were together. I primarily lived with my mom, except for a few weeks I'd spend in Washington, DC, with Dad."

The difference between Elk Valley, Wyoming, and Washington, DC, was like comparing the moon to the sun. "You didn't want to live in DC?"

"Not one little bit." She finished combining the ground

beef with taco seasoning then turned to face him. "I like it here."

Here at the ranch? No, she'd meant here in Elk Valley. "I can't imagine living in the big city. Too much traffic, too many people."

"Not enough wide-open spaces," she agreed. "Or mountains. I really love the mountains." She wrinkled her nose. "My mom keeps trying to get me to come to Arizona, but it's too hot there in the summer. Elk Valley is my home."

The urge to walk across the kitchen to pull her into his arms was strong. He tried to understand why he was so drawn to Ashley. It was more than her outward beauty. She had a sweet openness about her, not that she was naïve, but more that she seemed to accept people for who they were, regardless of their faults. And if he were honest, he'd admit he was touched by her faith, especially the way she prayed for him.

He liked her. She was incredibly easy to be around, no matter what they were doing.

"It must be hard on you, not having your family nearby." He sought her gaze.

"Sometimes." Her smile seemed sad. "I love both my parents, but it's not easy to divide my time between Arizona and DC, when I've made my life here."

"I miss my parents, too." Despite his determination to shield his heart, he found himself taking a step toward her. "Not having family to lean on in times of trouble can be difficult."

"Yes, that's it exactly." Her eyes clung to his. "Having someone to share your feelings, the good and the bad, is important."

"I couldn't agree more." He took another step closer, as if drawn to her by an invisible yet unbreakable thread.

"Cade." Her voice was a hushed whisper that did nothing to stop him. She held herself still, until he caught her hand and tugged her forward until she was in his arms.

Where she belonged.

He lowered his mouth, giving her plenty of time to say no. To draw back.

She didn't.

He kissed her, the tangy taco seasoning she must have tried earlier on her lips. The way she clung to him messed with his head.

But then she broke off their embrace, placing her hand on his chest. He imagined she could feel the way his heart pounded beneath her fingertips.

"We can't." Her voice sounded low and uneven. "I need to stay focused on the investigation. This—won't help."

Hard to argue the need to concentrate on uncovering the truth around Melissa's kidnapping, so he nodded and released her. He raked his fingers through his hair. "I'm sorry. I didn't mean to take advantage."

"You didn't." Her cheeks flushed and she quickly turned away to stand at the stove. "I, um, hope you're hungry. Dinner will be ready soon. I just need to cut up the tomatoes, lettuce and black olives. I already put the shredded cheese in a bowl."

"Great." He wanted more than just tacos but managed to keep his thoughts to himself. Ashley had kissed him back, but that didn't mean she was interested in starting something with him.

She could have anyone she wanted. Like one of those handsome cowboys. Although it seemed she'd tried that route in the past and it hadn't gone well.

Danny made a gurgling sound, drawing his attention. The little boy was awake, but not in distress. He waved his arms in jerky movements, as if unsure how they worked.

Danny appeared to be looking directly at him, his dark eyes intense.

This needed to be his focus, Cade told himself sternly as he crossed over to lift the baby into his arms. Danny and Melissa had to come first.

Always.

As he walked with Danny around the house, chattering nonsense, he tried not to dwell on how empty the house would feel once Ashley was gone.

Why on earth had she kissed him?

Ashley shook her head at her foolishness. Enough was enough; she needed to find a way to keep Cade in the friendship category.

Not as a potential guy she was interested in. Very interested in.

Stop it! Her brain shouted the words in her mind.

She pushed herself away from the counter, focusing on Ozzy. The K-9 hadn't interrupted their kiss this time, which she found unnerving. Did that mean the dog had come to like Cade as much as she did?

Oh, boy.

"I need to take Oz outside." She grabbed her coat. "Be back in a few."

Outside, she paused when she saw the horses in the field. They were graceful and beautiful, making her long to head out for a ride. Her childhood friend, Sissy, had owned several horses, so she had some experience with horses.

There was too much to like about being here at the ranch. She needed to remember this wasn't her world. She didn't belong here. She liked being a cop. And intended to prove herself to be a good one.

"Come, Ozzy," she called. "Let's walk."

Thick clouds hovered over the mountain, making the

hour seem later than it was. She took Ozzy around the ranch house, raking her eyes over the wooded area where the perp had taken a shot at her the night before.

All was quiet today, but she didn't find that reassuring. After attacking Cade in the barn, she felt certain this perp was out there, planning his next move.

She wanted to be prepared, mentally and physically, for whatever this guy tossed at them next. Ozzy seemed to be on alert, too.

"Good boy," she murmured as they finished walking around the house to head back inside. When they entered the kitchen, she was surprised to see Cade had set out all of the ingredients for their tacos, including the hard shells.

"Everything okay?" he asked.

It was all she could do not to tell him everything was perfect. "Yep, no sign of trouble."

"Good." He gestured toward the table. "Sit down, everything is ready."

She hung up her coat and then crossed to the end of the counter where she had set Ozzy's bucket of kibble.

On cue, Oz followed, sitting a few feet away, watching and waiting patiently as she filled his food and water dishes. Even when she set them down, he knew better than to immediately leap forward. She held his gaze then told him to go ahead, gesturing to the bowls.

That was all he needed to dart forward to eat.

"He's very well trained," Cade said as he cut up the lettuce.

"I had to be trained almost as much as he did," she confessed. "Scent training came naturally to him, but working as a team took some discipline." She grinned. "I couldn't ask for a better partner."

"It's amazing to watch you two." He prepared the olives as she cut up tomatoes. "Ready to eat?"

"Sure." Why did making a meal together feel like another type of teamwork?

As always, she was touched by Cade's faith as he prayed for God to continue watching over Melissa and to guide her and Ozzy to finding her. She added a silent prayer of her own, asking for God to provide Cade the strength he needed to keep the perp from getting close to Danny.

After dinner, Cade went out to bring the horses back into the barn. While he was gone, she kept an eye on Danny while continuing to work. She spoke to both Roger and Earl at the Rocking W. Both men hadn't even known about Melissa's kidnapping and seemed sincerely shocked at the news. Deciding that speaking to them again in person wasn't necessary, she was about to move on when Chase called to let her know she needed to report to the police station in the morning for the arrival of Cowgirl. She quickly agreed, anxious to see the beautiful labradoodle herself.

That night, she and Cade took turns staying on guard. Considering the gunman's attempt to get Cade in the barn, Nora had agreed to have an officer sit outside again, too.

Something Ashley knew probably wouldn't happen in a bigger city. Their small police department resources were stretched, but she admired Nora for prioritizing the safety of their citizens. Especially an innocent baby.

The following morning, she and Cade fell into the same routine. She watched Danny and cooked breakfast while Cade did the early morning chores.

"We need to head into Elk Valley for a while this morning," she informed him when they were finished eating. "I'd like you and Danny to come with me."

He frowned. "Has there been a break in the case?"

"Not exactly. We have a therapy dog that has been donated to the task force. Our trainer, Liana Lightfoot, is going to adopt Cowgirl, but she will be used by anyone in the team who sees a need."

He quirked a brow. "You think I need Cowgirl's expertise?"

He was joking, but she held his gaze. "It couldn't hurt. You're going through a difficult time with being Danny's caretaker while your sister is missing. Why not meet the labradoodle?"

"I'm fine. Her services are better used by those who are struggling."

Was it the macho rancher in him that had him loathe to show weakness? Maybe, but she knew that no matter what Cade said, he would enjoy meeting Cowgirl. "Either way, we still need to stick together. If our small town department had more resources, I'd ask for another officer to swing by. But we're stretched pretty thin at the moment."

"Okay." He smiled and shrugged. "I'm used to this by now. I'll pack Danny's diaper bag."

As before, she insisted on taking her SUV because of Ozzy's special compartment in the back. The sun was bright this morning, the clouds from the night before having dissipated. She glanced at Cade curiously. "What would you be doing if you didn't need to stay with me and Danny?"

"I need to move my cattle soon." He gestured to the brightness. "This would be a perfect day for that. Takes several hours, though, especially if I'm doing the work alone."

She'd sensed he was holding back from doing major chores in Melissa's absence, and his comment proven it. "I'm sorry for the delay. I'm sure we'll find your sister soon."

He nodded, but didn't say anything more. She couldn't blame him for feeling a bit hopeless. She struggled to stay positive, too.

When they arrived at the Elk Valley police station, Cade

reluctantly followed her and Ozzy inside. There was no sign of Cowgirl yet, so Cade went over to his usual chair along the wall, setting Danny's infant seat beside him.

"Oh, Ashley, there you are." Tech Analyst Isla Jimenez came out of the conference room. "I have a report on those two potential suspects you wanted me to look into."

"Anything interesting pop up?"

Isla shook her head. "No, sorry, they're both clean." Ashley noticed Isla's eyes move toward Cade and Danny. Cade had taken the baby from his carrier and removed his snowsuit. Ashely noticed the infant was spending more time awake and taking in his surroundings, which must have caught Isla's attention. "Ohhh. The baby is so precious."

"Yes, he is." She eyed Isla curiously. The wistful expression on her face was something new. She placed a hand on the tech specialist's arm. "Hey, are you okay?"

"I…uh." Isla tore her gaze from Danny with an effort. "I'm fine. A few days ago I received the news that I've been approved as a foster mother."

"Congratulations." Ashley smiled. She knew Isla had grown up in the foster system herself, and that the young woman wanted to have a baby of her own. Isla was only four years older than Ashley. "I'm thrilled for you, Isla."

"Thanks." Isla's dark eyes brightened with anticipation. "Even more exciting is that there's a baby girl named Charisse who may need a home in the next few days. Unfortunately, her mother abandoned her, and the department of health and human services is involved in finding temporary placement for her."

That aspect of the process didn't sound good. "I'm sorry to hear about Charisse's mother, but it's good that you're ready and willing to take over."

"Yes. That's been the hard part of going through the training to be a foster parent." A small frown furrowed

Isla's brow. "I don't like the different circumstances that cause a baby to end up in the foster care system, but I hope and pray I'm ready to help those in need."

"You'll be great." Ashley hesitated then felt compelled to ask, "Do both Chase and Nora know?"

"Yes, they're okay with it. I've promised to keep working even after the baby has been placed in my care. Thankfully, my grandmother has agreed to help me, too."

"That sounds good." She knew Isla's talents were needed on the task force, but obviously, being a foster mother was important to her. And Ashley was secretly impressed that Chase had been so accommodating. It seemed as if her presence on the task force was the only thing he'd objected to, thanks to her dad's interference. Hopefully, Cowgirl's arrival would smooth things over.

She gestured to Cade and Danny. "I know from personal experience that newborns sleep a lot. They also eat a lot, so be prepared for frequent feedings."

"Trust me, I've read every baby book in the Elk Valley library," Isla confided. She reached into her pocket to pull out her cell phone. "Would you like to see Charisse's picture?"

"Of course." Ashley peered over Isla's shoulder as she tapped the screen. An adorable olive-skinned infant with dark eyes stared back at her. "Oh, Isla, she's beautiful."

"I think so, too." Isla gazed at the photo then glanced at Cade and Danny. She slowly lowered the phone, tucking it back into her pocket. "Finding the right man hasn't been my path, unfortunately. Yet there's no denying there's just something about a big strong man holding a baby that makes me melt inside."

Until recently, Ashley would have pooh-poohed the idea. She'd been focused on her career, especially after the months she'd spent training to become a K-9 officer.

Even more so when she'd been asked to join the multia-gency task force.

Yet things were different now that she'd spent the past forty-eight hours with Cade and Danny. Living with them.

Bonding with them.

Isla was right. There was something very compelling about watching Cade interact with his nephew.

The same way he'd care for a child of his own.

TWELVE

Swallowing his impatience, Cade held Danny as Ashley followed up with members of her team. When the precinct door opened, his attention was diverted to a woman with long dark hair crossing the threshold. She led a brown, curly-haired labradoodle inside, the dog looking around with lively interest in her surroundings.

"Hi, everyone. Meet Cowgirl!" She gestured to the dog with a wide smile.

"Liana, she's adorable!" Ashley hurried over to meet them. The labradoodle wiggled with happiness, licking at Ashley's hand, making her laugh.

Cade found himself smiling, too. Just watching the playful dog eased his annoyance. And made him realize how much he missed Skippy, the border collie he'd lost early last year. The more time he spent with Ashley and Ozzy, the more he thought about getting another dog. Sooner than later.

"Do you mind if I bring Cowgirl over to meet Cade and Danny?" Ashley asked. Ozzy and Cowgirl appeared enamored of each other during their brief meeting.

"Of course not." Liana handed over the leash. "We have you to thank for Cowgirl's arrival in the first place."

He hadn't realized Ashley had been the one responsible for the therapy dog. She brought the labradoodle over to where he sat with Danny, keeping Ozzy on her other side.

Cowgirl nuzzled the baby, her tail wagging. Up close, he could see the dark brown splotch on her right ear.

"You're a good girl, aren't you?" He sank his fingers into her brown curls. Then he looked up at Ashley. "It was a great idea for you to arrange Cowgirl to be brought here."

Her cheeks flushed and she shrugged. "Seeing the grief reflected in the victims' families made me want to provide an emotional support dog for them. I asked my dad, Brian Hanson, Bureau Chief in the Washington FBI office, for a favor, hoping the FBI would approve the concept. They didn't, but my dad paid for Cowgirl himself."

Interesting. He looked down at the dog again, hating to admit he'd never thought much of the idea of having an emotional support dog. But the way Cowgirl had cheered him up had proven he wasn't as immune to the need as he'd thought. "I think she'll make a great addition to the team."

"There she is." A tall man Cade recognized as FBI agent, and Rocky Mountain Killer task force leader, Chase Rawlston, stepped from the conference room to join them. "What do you think, Liana? Getting Cowgirl acclimated to our environment shouldn't be too difficult, right?"

"Not at all," Liana assured him. "She's a natural and, of course, has had extensive training already. I'm going to work on bonding with her for a few days before using her with victims' families."

Cade noticed Chase's gaze darted toward Ashley.

"Guess your dad came through for you again."

Ashley lifted her chin. "Not again. The only favor I've asked of my father is for this emotional support dog. Nothing else."

Chase stared at her for a moment then gave a short nod and turned away. "Take care of the newest member of our team, Liana."

"Come, Cowgirl." Liana took the dog's leash and headed

back outside. Based on Chase's comments, Cade assumed she was the team's dog trainer.

Chase disappeared into the conference room, leaving Ashley staring after him, her frustration clearly etched on her face.

Then she bent and stroked Ozzy's fur, as if needing a moment to pull herself together.

"Are you okay?" Cade asked in a low tone.

"Fine." Her smile didn't quite reach her eyes. "I need to get some information from Isla, our tech analyst, then we can go."

"Okay, sounds good." He watched as Ashley crossed over to speak with another pretty woman with brown hair and light brown eyes, who appeared to be enamored of Danny.

"Isla, will you send me those reports you created on our newest suspects? I'd like to look at them more closely."

"Of course. I'll email them right away."

"Thanks." Ashley turned to face him. "I'm ready, if you are?"

He nodded. "Give me a minute to get Danny bundled up." As he had the process down to a science, it didn't take long to zip Danny into his snowsuit then strap him into the car seat. He had to admit, a baby was more work than a dog.

Well, maybe not more work than a puppy.

Ashley led the way outside, holding the door for him. Ozzy craned his neck, as if searching for Cowgirl.

Once they were seated in Ashley's SUV, she backed out of the parking lot. "Sounds like Chase thought you asked your dad to be included on the task force."

"I didn't." Her denial was swift. "I would never do something like that. That was my dad's idea, I didn't even realize he'd poked his nose into the situation until Chase said something."

"I'm sure your dad was just looking out for you."

She snorted. "More like trying to make up for the years he was gone from my life."

Ouch, he thought. "You mentioned the divorce earlier, but I can see how difficult it must have been to have an absentee father."

She shrugged. "You can't miss what you didn't have." She glanced at him, her expression wry. "I was so excited to have been included in the task force, until I realized Chase was less than thrilled to have me on the team. I know he thinks I've wormed my way in. All I can do now is to prove that Ozzy and I are good at what we do. And that we're an asset for the team."

"You are," he assured her. "I'm impressed with Ozzy's tracking ability."

She nodded, looking unconvinced. He tried to think of something more to say that would help, but came up blank.

Silence hung between them on the ride to the ranch. He scanned the area outside the house, thankfully finding nothing unusual or suspicious.

Ashley parked and then shut down the engine. "I'll watch Danny while you get caught up on chores."

"I'd appreciate that." Her offer was heartwarming. "He's been fed recently, so you should have time to get some work done."

"I'm counting on it," she said with a smile.

They headed into the ranch house. He led the way with Danny, while Ashley and Ozzy covered his back. It went against the grain to have her putting herself in harm's way, but there was nothing he could do to change the fact that Danny needed to be protected at all costs.

He took Danny out of his snowsuit, grimacing when he realized the baby had spit up on the garment and the side of his infant seat. Carefully picking up the sleeping baby, he carried him down the hall to his master bedroom, where he'd left Danny's bassinet. He set the sleeping baby inside, then frowned, realizing he'd need to throw a load of laundry in and clean up the mess before he could head out to the barn.

He'd just returned to the kitchen when his phone chimed with an incoming text. Surprised, he glanced down at the device.

Melissa's name flashed on the screen. His hand shot out to grab Ashley's arm. "I have a text from Melissa!"

Ashley stepped up beside him. "Let me see."

Bring Danny to the abandoned cabin east of your ranch within fifteen minutes or I'll kill Melissa.

He stared at the message, a sinking feeling in his chest. He turned the phone toward her. "It's not Melissa. It's from her kidnapper."

Ashley scanned the text, her brow furrowed. "Isolated cabin? Yeah, right. It's a trap."

"I figured that out for myself." His fingers tightened on the phone. "But I need to go. Right now!"

"Hold on, Cade. Let me think about this." Ashley reached out to put a hand over the phone screen. "We can't just rush off without a plan. We need backup to make this work. And we need a doll to use as a decoy. It's going to take some time to get everything arranged."

"We don't have time." He bit back a flash of irritation. "He only gave us fifteen minutes before he hurts my sister!"

"Yes, that's what he's demanding. But you need to text back saying you want proof Melissa is alive and unharmed before you come." Ashley's voice was calm. "Think about it, Cade. How do you know he didn't hurt Melissa already?"

She had a point. He struggled to breathe as he quickly texted back.

Send proof Melissa is unharmed or no deal.

Behind him, he could hear Ashley using her phone to make the necessary arrangements for backup. He appreciated her efforts, but feared it would be too little too late.

He'd make a doll by sticking rolled clothing into another one of Danny's snowsuits and strapping it into the car seat. Because waiting wasn't an option.

He was going to get Melissa home safe.

No matter what.

He stared at his phone, holding his breath as the three little dots indicated a response would be forthcoming.

Hang on, Melissa, he thought. *I'm coming for you!*

The way Cade's body vibrated with tension was concerning. Ashley knew he would take off on his own without backup.

"Hurry," she urged Nora. "We don't have a lot of time."

"Understood." Nora ended the call.

"Cade, did you get proof Melissa is alive and well?" She needed him to focus.

"Not yet." His voice was strained. "Every minute is agony."

"I know. But it's necessary."

His phone chimed and, if anything, his expression grew even more worried. He turned the device to show her the response.

Take my word for it.

"No, Cade. That's not good enough." She glanced down

at Ozzy, who was sitting beside her. His dark stare seemed to indicate he knew something was wrong. "Insist on talking to Melissa."

He nodded and used his phone to call her. Within seconds, she could tell the call had been sent to voice mail. Cade's thumbs danced on the screen as he sent another text.

Nora had informed her that the two officers out on patrol were on the other side of town, but would be heading to the ranch shortly. Ashley desperately wanted them to get there ASAP. Cade wasn't about to wait much longer.

In a way, she couldn't blame him.

Ozzy lifted his head, his ears perked. She wondered what may have caught his attention then heard a soft noise. A mewling sound. An animal, like a stray cat?

The abrupt retort of gunfire had her reaching for Cade and dragging him away from the front door. Two seconds later, the door burst open. A man stepped over the threshold, dragging a dark-haired woman with him. He held a Smith & Wesson handgun pressed tightly against her temple.

"You want proof?" the man snarled in a nasally voice. "Here's your proof. She's alive. But not for long."

Cade shook off Ashley's grasp and stepped forward. "Vincent. I should have known it was you. I don't understand. Why are you doing this? I'm sure a DNA test will prove you're Danny's father. And of course you would have visitation rights to the baby."

"No! Don't let him touch Danny!" Melissa sobbed, her face pale. Then she cried out in pain as Vincent dug the barrel of the gun deeper into her temple.

"Shut up!" Vincent was so irate, spittle flew from his mouth. "I don't care about DNA or visitation rights. I want the kid! Now! Or you're all going to die!"

The kid? It was an odd way to talk about his son. Ashley had a bad feeling about what Vincent intended to do with the baby. She also feared Cade would throw himself at Vincent if he thought he could take the guy down.

She eased to the side, giving Ozzy the hand signal to stay so he wouldn't get hurt. She moved cautiously so as not to draw Vincent's attention. She needed a clear path toward him if the situation continued spiraling out of control.

"Okay, I'll get Danny for you," Cade said, his tone even. "But you need to put the gun away first."

"No!" Vincent roared in anger, his voice reverberating through the room. "I have the gun and I'm calling the shots! Give me the kid!"

The screaming must have woken Danny because he began to cry. Instantly, Vincent's attention shifted away from her and Cade to the hallway leading to the bedrooms.

"Never mind. I'll get him." Vincent took several steps into the hallway, dragging Melissa with him. He still had the gun pressed so tightly against her temple, Ashley feared he'd draw blood from the pressure.

"Stop, please," Melissa whimpered.

Ashley pulled her weapon, despite the fact there was no clear shot that wouldn't endanger Melissa.

Cade took a step toward Vincent, too, as if intending to follow. Without warning, Melissa thrust her elbow up and back, smacking Vincent sharply in the face. The guy howled, blood spurting from his nose.

Melissa wrenched free as Cade launched himself at Vincent. His long arms managed to grab Vincent's gun hand, twisting with such force that the weapon broke free.

With a shriek of rage, Vincent grabbed the lamp from the nearby table and threw it at Cade. Ashley darted forward, desperate for a clear shot, but Cade and Melissa were in her way. Vincent disappeared down the hallway.

"Danny!" Melissa screamed her son's name, adding to

the chaos. She rushed directly into Ashley's line of fire, heading straight to the sound of her baby's crying.

Cade jumped over the lamp, blood running down his temple from where he'd been struck. He dashed along the hallway, veering around Melissa as she entered the master suite to pick up her son, his gaze focused on the escape path Vincent had taken through the house.

"Stay back, he's armed," Ashley shouted, even as gunfire rang out, causing Cade to hit the floor outside Melissa's room.

"I have Danny," Melissa called in a trembling voice.

Ozzy growled and barked, but stayed at her side the way he was trained to do. He wasn't trained in suspect apprehension, so she didn't dare send him after Vincent.

There was a screeching sound, indicating a window was being opened. Ashley hugged the wall as she made her way down the hall.

"Stay down, Cade." She didn't want him in her way. When she reached Melissa's bedroom, she paused and quickly peeked around the open doorway, bracing herself for more gunfire.

The room was empty!

"Ozzy, come!" Ashley didn't want Vincent to get away. She ran to the open window, but didn't see him. Had he already reached the trees? The sound of wailing sirens indicated her backup was on the way. Reassured, she threw her leg over the windowsill. Once outside, she urged Ozzy to join her.

The black Lab gracefully jumped down from the window. At least Vincent hadn't broken it, leaving glass shards around. "Seek!" she said, giving Ozzy the general command. She couldn't use the glove scent, as she wasn't sure the glove had been left behind by Vincent.

Ozzy dropped his nose to the ground, sniffing around

the area outside the window, before trotting toward the woods. She kept pace with her K-9, searching for Vincent among the brush.

It was dangerous to follow an armed man, but she pushed forward, unwilling to let him get away. Thankfully, Ozzy was still wearing his bullet-resistant K-9 vest.

Her K-9 quickly reached the woods, still hot on the trail. Ducking beneath tree branches, and pushing through brush, she followed, weapon in hand.

A glimpse of movement off to the right caught her attention. "Ozzy, down!"

Her K-9 dropped to his belly while she ducked behind a tree. The crack of gunfire had her heart in her throat. Crouched low, she scanned the horizon, her eyes landing on an outcropping of rock.

Feeling sick, she realized Vincent was using the rock as protection while the higher elevation gave him a perfect view of the terrain below.

Including her and Ozzy.

"Stay down, boy," she called softly. "Stay down."

She forced herself to wait for several long agonizing moments before she crept out from behind the tree and darted toward her K-9.

When she reached Oz, she covered him with her body, her heart pounding erratically in her chest. She felt along his soft fur, reassuring herself he hadn't been hit.

"Good boy," she whispered, flattening herself to the ground as much as possible without squishing her dog. Being reunited with him helped calm her ragged nerves.

The seconds turned to one minute. Then two. Still no sound of gunfire, or any sign of Vincent. Had she lost him? Everything inside her railed at the possibility.

After five minutes, she pushed herself to her hands and

knees. Hearing movement behind her, she glanced over her shoulder.

"Ashley? Are you okay?" She was surprised to see Chase Rawlston himself crossing the open area between the ranch house and the woods. He looked strong and competent, his dark eyes intense. His K-9, a golden retriever named Dash, was at his side. The dog's coat was several shades lighter than Chase's brown hair. She inwardly groaned, wishing she could have thrust a cuffed Vincent toward her boss, rather than be hiding in the brush from him.

"Stay back," she warned. "Gunman is positioned behind a rock above me."

Chase ducked to a crouch and moved forward with Dash until he was also in the woods. His movement was enough to have drawn gunfire, but there was nothing but silence.

"He may have taken off," she said in a low voice.

"We'll check it out." Chase waved a hand to the left. "I'll go this way, you take the other side."

"Understood." She rose to her feet. "Ozzy, heel."

The dog positioned himself along the side of her leg. She made a wide berth so that she could approach the outcropping of rock from the side.

There was hardly any sound as she and Chase approached from opposite sides of the woods. The closer they got, the more she was convinced Vincent had escaped.

After cresting the hill, she stopped. "He's gone," she said in a voice loud enough to reach Chase.

There was the sound of scrambling footsteps as Chase and Dash appeared on the other side, directly across from her. His expression was solemn as it held hers. "Let's see if we can find the spent shell casing."

"Seek, Ozzy." She gave her K-9 the command to move closer. He loped up to the wide flat area behind the rock, nose to the ground. Then he abruptly sat and looked at her. She hurried over to see what he'd found.

"Got it," she said with satisfaction.

"Great. Bag it, Hanson."

She removed an evidence bag from her pocket and carefully picked up the shell casing. It was similar in size and caliber to the one Ozzy had found the other day.

"Should I take Ozzy and keep following his trail?" she asked Chase.

"No, it's too dangerous." Chase grimaced. "At least we know who we're looking for. Best to get back to the house for now."

"Okay. The good news is that Melissa and Danny are safe."

Chase nodded. "That's the most important thing."

As she turned and headed back down the hill, she knew Chase was right about how great it was to have Melissa and Danny reunited.

But it wasn't easy to hide her keen disappointment over allowing Vincent to get away.

THIRTEEN

"**M**elissa, tell me what happened. Are you okay? Did Vincent hurt you?" After cleaning up the mess from the broken lamp and providing a temporary fix to the front door that Vincent had fired through, nailing it shut so that they'd be safe, Cade sat near his sister on the sofa. Melissa hadn't set Danny down once since going into the master bedroom to keep him safe.

"I'm fine." She sniffed, her gaze clinging to her infant son. "The only thing that kept me going was knowing you'd keep Danny safe."

It wrenched his heart to see her looking so fragile. Her pale skin contrasted with the dark circles under her eyes. Her long dark hair appeared dull and listless from her time in captivity. He wanted to ask more, but there was a knock at the back door. He crossed over to let Ashley, Ozzy, Chase and his golden retriever, Dash, to enter the house. The fact they didn't have Vincent in cuffs was depressing.

"We lost him," Ashley said, reading his mind. "I'm sorry, Cade. He fired at us from a hiding spot behind a rock, making it difficult to keep tracking him."

He shifted his glance to Ozzy, understanding the danger. "I don't blame you. I know you and Ozzy did your best. I'm glad neither of you was hurt."

"We're okay. I need to talk to Melissa." Ashley looked past him to where his sister was seated. "She may know where we can find Vincent."

"I'm going to call Nora, give her the update," Chase said. "Go ahead and interview Ms. McNeal."

"Thanks." Ashley took a moment to remove Ozzy's K-9 vest, then offered him fresh water before moving to the sofa. Cade dropped into the chair to Ashley's right, intending to be there to support his sister.

"Ms. McNeal? I'm Elk Valley police officer Ashley Hanson, and this is my K-9 partner, Ozzy."

"Please call me Melissa." She offered a wan smile as she looked from Ashley to the dog. "It's nice to meet you."

"Likewise, and you may call me Ashley. I'm so glad you're home safe." Ashley's warmth was palpable. "I know you've been through a terrible ordeal, but I need to understand what happened. If you could start at the beginning, that would help."

Melissa's eyes darted to him then returned to Ashley. "Vincent called me from a strange number. He claimed he had a new job and that he was using his new work phone."

Cade's stomach knotted. He'd known Melissa had been acting strange before the kidnapping, but he wished he'd pressed for information.

Or that his sister would have trusted him enough to share the news that Vincent had popped back into her life.

"Go on," Ashley encouraged.

"Vince wanted to see Danny, but I was hesitant." This time his sister turned to face him. "I'm sorry, Cade. I should have told you, especially since I sensed that Vincent wasn't being entirely truthful. He kept stressing that he had rights as Danny's father, and I was worried he'd take me to court for custody. I thought talking to him might help."

"I'm not angry with you, sis." He offered a reassuring smile. "All that matters is that you and Danny are safe."

Her expression turned grim and she stared down at

Danny for a long moment. "We won't be safe until Vincent is behind bars."

"What happened after Vincent reached out?" Ashley asked. "How did he get you to the park?"

Melissa dragged in a calming breath. "I asked Cade to take Danny to the store because I wanted to talk to Vincent alone. He thought I was bringing Danny and was incensed when he came to the ranch house and discovered I didn't have the baby."

Cade lifted his heart in prayer, thanking God for keeping Danny safe. "I'm glad I was able to help that day."

"Vincent hit me on the head outside the house. The next thing I knew, I was tied up to a tree in the woods outside the park." Her voice hitched at the memory. "I was shocked, but knew Danny was in danger."

"Ozzy found the tree and rope," Ashley said, stroking the black Lab's silky fur. "He's an excellent tracker. How did you get away?"

Melissa shook her head. "Honestly? I'm not sure. I wiggled around, tugging and pulling at my wrists until the ropes loosened." She glanced at him again. "You always mentioned having faith in God, and I prayed the entire time, Cade. More than at any other time in my entire life."

"I'm glad to hear it." His voice came out low and husky. He knew God had been watching over Melissa, and Danny, too. "God is always there for us, Melissa."

"I believe that," she murmured. "After I freed myself from the bindings, I ran back to the parking lot. I saw the ski-masked man coming after you, so I shouted for you to keep Danny safe. He chased you, Cade, but then turned around and grabbed me, shoving me into the van."

"Who was driving the van?" Ashley asked.

Melissa's brow creased. "Vincent was driving. I don't know who the masked man was. Once I was in the van, I was drugged with some sedative. When I woke up, I was in an old cabin, tied to a cot, with only a wood-burning stove to stay warm."

The news was disappointing, and he exchanged looks with Ashley. "You were in this cabin the entire time since the kidnapping?"

"Yes." Melissa shivered and hugged Danny closer. "Vincent would bring me food sometimes. He kept the ropes really tight because of the way I escaped near the park."

Cade had noticed the raw abrasions around Melissa's wrists. He didn't condone violence but curled his fingers into fists, wishing for another chance to deck Vincent.

"Do you have any idea what Vincent wanted with Danny?" Ashley asked. "Was this about taking full custody of his son?"

Melissa was shaking her head before Ashley finished asking the question. "No. That was the worst part of all. Vincent owes money to some loan shark." She raised her eyes to meet his. "He planned to kidnap Danny and to sell him on the black market."

Cade sucked in a harsh breath. "He told you that?"

"He taunted me with it," Melissa corrected bitterly. "Said the kid was going to bring him megabucks. Enough to pay his debt and to start over."

Ashley leaned forward. "Did Vincent say he had a buyer set up? And where this exchange would happen?"

"No. He just kept saying he'd be a rich man when this was over." Melissa shivered. "I knew that once he had Danny, Vincent planned to kill me."

"He'll never hurt you again," Cade said quickly. "You and Danny are safe now."

"I know." Her voice had dropped to a mere whisper. "I hate what Vincent has done, but I can't regret the fact that we made Danny. He's the best thing that's ever happened to me."

Cade knew what she meant. Without Vincent, Danny wouldn't exist. The baby was innocent, and a blessing in every way. Yet his father was also full of evil, planning to sell his own son to the highest bidder.

"God always has a plan for us," Ashley said. "You should stay focused on what is important, like taking care of your son."

"Yes, you're right. I need to remember this is all a part of God's plan." Melissa bent to press a kiss to the top of Danny's head.

"Is there anything else you remember to help us find Vincent?" Ashley prompted. "Think back over your conversations, however brief. Did he indicate where he was staying? Who he might be with?"

"He's not in the apartment over the garage," Cade added. "Ashley and Ozzy checked the place out the first night you were taken."

"And Ozzy didn't alert on Vincent's scent outside the van," Ashley said thoughtfully. "Makes me think Vincent had someone else tie you up to the tree. The same accomplice must have dropped the glove and been the one to shove you into the van."

"That could be," Melissa agreed. "I'm sorry, but Vince never said where he was staying or who he was working with. I wish he had. I know he's not going to give up so easily."

A wave of helplessness washed over Cade. He wanted to lock Melissa and Danny somewhere safe where Vincent would never find them.

But where? And how?

"I'll call my neighbor, Roger Ward, at the Rocking W

Ranch. He'll help keep an eye on my livestock while I take you and Danny somewhere safe."

"We have a safe house for them," Chase said, entering the room. "I just finished making the arrangements with Chief Quan. We think it's best if we have an armed officer watching Melissa and Danny. We may need you, Cade, to help draw this Vincent guy out of hiding."

He was torn between wanting to help find Vincent and the need to be the one to personally keep his sister and nephew safe. He glanced at Melissa, who nodded. "I think you should help them, Cade. Danny and I will be fine with an armed officer watching over us."

Would they? He desperately wanted to believe that. He sought Ashley's gaze, seeking reassurance.

She smiled gently. "I agree with Chase. We'll get Melissa and Danny stashed away, and look for ways to draw Vincent or his partner out of hiding."

"Okay." He nodded slowly in agreement, secretly hoping and praying he wasn't making a huge mistake.

Ashley was surprised that Chase had already discussed moving Melissa and Danny to a safe house. She gave him a nod of thanks, which he returned.

"Did Nora have a destination in mind?" Ashley asked.

"No, but I do. There's a place the Feds have used in the past that will suit our needs." Chase gestured toward Melissa and the baby. "You may want to pack a few things in case you need to stay for a few days."

"A few days?" Cade echoed in protest.

"We need time to come up with a plan." Chase turned to Ashley. "It's best if you take Melissa, Danny and Cade to the safe house in your vehicle, I'll stay close behind, to make sure we're not followed."

"That works." She rose. "Melissa, do you need help getting packed?"

"No, I can do it." Her expression was troubled as she stood and carried Danny down the hall.

"I hope this is the right way to go." Cade jammed his fingers into his hair. "She just came home and now we're shipping her off again."

"To keep her safe," Ashley gently reminded. "Hopefully, we'll find Vincent and his accomplice very soon. Then you'll be reunited once and for all."

"Yeah. I know. I need to have faith." He sighed. "I guess Elaine isn't involved, after all."

"Probably not. While we don't know who Vincent's accomplice is, I think Melissa would have been able to figure out if the person was a woman."

"Ashley?" Chase caught her attention. "I need to show you the location of the safe house. It's located on the complete opposite side of town from here."

She hurried over to where he had a sheet of paper on the table. With a pen, he wrote the address then drew a map of the area. "The place is here, it's a two-story home with brown-cedar siding." He marked the place with an X.

Searching her memory, she nodded. "I know where it is. It's a drive, though. Will take a half hour to get there from here."

"Yep. But at least Vincent and his accomplice won't know they're staying there." Chase shrugged. "The chief is sending Officer Ed Gerund to be on guard."

"Okay." Gerund had plenty of years of experience under his belt. She was secretly glad Chase hadn't stuck her on guard duty, the way she'd expected he might, given her rookie status within the department. Then again, they may need Ozzy's keen nose to track Vincent. "We'll hit the road once Melissa and Danny are ready. Oh, and what about food?"

"The place is stocked with the basics, including frozen pizzas. By the way, you and Ozzy did great work today." Chase's praise seemed sincere. "I was impressed at how well you and your partner were able to track our perp."

"Thanks." She tried not to show just how much his comments meant to her. "Ozzy is a natural when it comes to scent tracking."

"I can see that. And the two of you have an amazing bond." Chase handed her the map and turned away. "I'll be outside, waiting for you and the others. I want to clear the area to make sure this guy didn't double back to try again."

"Thanks. Uh, Chase?" He paused at the doorway, glancing back at her. "Why are you involved in this? It's a local crime, not associated with our task force."

"The Feds are always involved in infant abductions. The minute we knew the baby was the ultimate target, I asked Nora to keep me involved and updated. It's also why I wanted you to take the lead."

"I see." She was ashamed for thinking the worst about Chase. That he'd sidelined her from the task force because of her father and her lack of experience. "I'm glad you are involved, as Vincent's plan was to sell the baby to the highest bidder."

"I heard." Chase's eyes darkened with anger. "Despicable. We need to get him, and soon."

She couldn't agree more.

After Chase left with Dash, Cade came over to stand beside her. "I feel the need to ask what your plan is once we drop off Melissa and Danny. I, uh…are you going to stay here for the night?"

She felt herself blush, even though he'd been nothing but a gentleman. "I would like to stay, as it's possible Vincent will return very soon to try again. He may assume that Melissa and Danny will still be here."

"Thank you. While I can protect myself, I'm sure Vincent will return at some point." His scowl deepened. "Better for us to stick together. It improves our chances of taking him down. And I'd like to know more about this plan to draw Vincent out of hiding."

She was curious about Chase's and Nora's thoughts on that, too, but didn't mention it. "First, we get Melissa and Danny to safety."

"Agreed." Cade turned away when Melissa came out of the bedroom, Danny's diaper bag slung over her shoulder.

She noticed Melissa had taken the time to change into fresh clothes. The way Melissa's eyes darted toward the fridge, gave her an inkling that she was hungry.

"Chase mentioned there are frozen pizzas at the safe house," she said. "If you need something to munch on in the meantime, help yourself."

"I'm fine until we get there." She lifted Danny's car seat and set it on the table. "He seems heavier than when I left."

"I'll take him." Cade donned his rawhide coat and cowboy hat, then reached for the car seat. "You're tired and weak, Melissa. A few good meals and a decent night's sleep, and you'll feel better."

"I hope so." Her gaze lingered on the baby. "I can't tell you how much I missed Danny. Even though he's a lot of work, I hated being apart from him."

"You're a good mom," Cade assured her. "And I'm sure you're hungry. There's string cheese in the fridge. Grab some for the ride."

"Okay." Melissa set the diaper bag aside, pulled two sticks of string cheese from the fridge, then shrugged into her coat. Ashley and Ozzy went outside first. She raked her eyes over the area, noticing that Chase and Dash were standing near her SUV. He gave her a nod, so she moved forward, holding the door for the others.

Minutes later, they were settled in the SUV. Chase gestured for her to pull out first. Imagining his hastily drawn map in her mind, she took the highway toward town.

In the back seat, Melissa hovered over Danny's car seat, as if needing to watch him sleep. Ashley remembered a line of questioning she still needed to have with Melissa, and caught her gaze in the rearview mirror. Now that she knew for sure Vincent was involved, her thoughts went back to his best friend.

"Melissa, is it possible that Vincent's friend, Rafe Travon, was involved in the kidnapping? Could he have been the other masked man?"

The young woman thought about that for a moment. "Maybe, but Rafe usually smells like tobacco and I didn't get that scent from the guy in the van." She sighed. "I was only in there for a minute before they drugged me."

"Rafe smokes cigarettes? Or chews tobacco?"

"Both." Melissa wrinkled her nose with distaste. "Mostly cigarettes, from what I remember. I hated it when Rafe and Vince hung out together, because Vince would sometimes join him in smoking."

"Ashley, do you think Ozzy can track the scent of tobacco?" Cade asked.

"He can, but it's better for him to be focused on an individual's scent. Labs like Ozzy can hold up to one hundred million individual scents in his mind. That's much better because many people smoke cigarettes."

"One hundred million," Melissa repeated in awe. "That's amazing."

It was wrong to be prideful, but Ashley couldn't help showcasing Ozzy's amazing ability. "It is."

The conversation lagged as they slowed down to navigate the city streets. When driving past the park, she noticed Cade staring at it with a thoughtful expression.

Chase's safe house was another fifteen minutes from town. When she finally pulled into the driveway, she was relieved to see that Officer Gerund was already there. He stood waiting outside, the car in the driveway must have been his personal vehicle so as not to announce there was an officer on the premises.

"Looks nice," Melissa murmured.

Ashley sensed she was apprehensive, and hoped Officer Gerund would be able to reassure her they were safe here. Cade pushed out of the vehicle to help Melissa with Danny. Ashley joined Ed Gerund as Chase pulled in behind her SUV.

"This place will work great," Ed said. "I walked around the property. There are alarms on the windows and plenty of motion-sensor lights."

"It's well equipped to keeping people safe," Chase said.

It didn't take long for Melissa and Danny to get settled.

Danny woke up crying, so Ed offered to make the pizza while Melissa cared for the baby.

Cade gave his sister a tight hug when Ashley announced it was time to go. On the drive back to the ranch, he was unusually quiet.

"What's wrong?" She reached over to rest her hand on his arm. "I hope you're not worried about Melissa and Danny."

"No, it's not that." He sighed and covered her hand with his. "I've harbored so much hatred toward Elaine, believing she was the behind this. Seems my anger might be misplaced. I'm not sure she's involved, after all."

"It's hard to know for sure." She mentally chastised herself for not keeping an open mind. Maybe she wanted Elaine to be involved because she'd broken up with Cade.

Had she let her personal feelings cloud her judgment? Oh, yeah. Big time.

Despite her best efforts not to become emotionally involved with Cade and his adorable nephew, she suddenly realized it was too late.

She cared, far too much. Yet she knew she couldn't allow herself to become distracted by Cade. Not now. Not when she needed to prove herself worthy of being included in the biggest case of her career.

FOURTEEN

When Ashley turned into his ranch driveway, Cade realized this was the first time that he'd be able to simply head out to do chores without worrying about Danny. It was a strange feeling and, weirdly, he missed the little guy.

To think he'd once took the ability to do chores for granted.

"I, uh, thought we could have pizza for dinner tonight, too." Ashley's voice was hesitant. "If that's okay with you?"

"Who doesn't like pizza?" He forced himself to remove his hand from hers to get out of the SUV. "I have a few things to do first, so maybe give me an hour?"

"No problem." She seemed subdued, and he wasn't sure what was troubling her.

He slid out of the passenger seat, waiting for her to free Ozzy from the back. "Hey, I hope you're not blaming yourself for Vincent getting away."

She grimaced. "I really wish I'd have gotten a hold of him, but Ozzy is a tracking K-9, he's not trained as a suspect apprehension dog. He'd protect me, but I don't know that he'd take down a perp. Especially one armed with a gun."

Cade agreed Ozzy would attack anyone who tried to hurt Ashley, but he understood what she meant. He bent to scratch the dog behind his ears. "I'm just relieved you and Ozzy are okay. Better to let Vincent go than to risk Ozzy being shot."

"That was exactly what I thought." Her smile didn't

reach her eyes. "I'm going to keep digging into various social media accounts while you get caught up with the animals."

"Sounds good." He fought the urge to pull her close for a long hug and kiss. The way he'd often witnessed between his parents when his dad headed out to work the ranch.

He needed to keep himself on track here. They weren't a couple, no matter how the situation seemed to indicate otherwise.

Melissa was safe, and so was Danny. His life would get back to normal once they figured out a way to draw Vincent out of hiding.

He walked with Ashley and Ozzy inside so he could grab his rifle. As long as Vincent was out there, he intended to remain vigilant. In a way, he secretly hoped the guy would show up again. This time, Cade would make sure he didn't escape.

Returning to the barn, he attended to his livestock. For the first time since Melissa's abduction, he found solace in working with the animals.

An hour later, he headed to the ranch house, his stomach rumbling with hunger. The tangy scent of pizza intermingled with garlic bread made his mouth water.

"Oh, good, I was just about to head out to find you," Ashley said. Ozzy swiftly came over to greet him, black tail waving madly. "I was hungry, so I cooked dinner."

"You read my mind," he teased. He gave Ozzy some well-deserved attention then washed his hands at the sink. Ashley pulled the extra-large pie from the oven, the cheese golden brown. The garlic bread came out next. "Looks delicious."

"It's only frozen pizza and garlic bread, but I know what you mean." Ashley set the pizza in the center of the table and sliced it into triangles. She cut the garlic bread in two, too. Ozzy stretched out at her feet. He was well trained enough not to try to beg for table food. She quirked a brow. "I had to laugh when I saw you stocked jumbo-sized pizzas."

"Hey, ranching works up an appetite." He joined her at the kitchen table and then reached out to take her hand. "Ashley, we have so much to be grateful for."

"We do," she agreed solemnly.

He bowed his head. "Dear Lord Jesus, we thank You for this food we are about to eat. We also thank You for keeping Melissa safe in Your care, and reuniting her with Danny. We ask that You continue to guide us on the path of seeking justice, so that others can be safe from harm, too. Amen."

"Amen," Ashley echoed.

For a few minutes, there was only silence as they dug into their meals. The pizza was too hot, so he made quick work of the garlic bread.

"I discovered that Rafe Travon, Mike Stucky, Stuart Berg and Joe Jurgen are all friends with Vincent on social media."

"All of them?" He stared at her. "That seems unusual."

"Maybe not, if they were all part of the rodeo circuit at some point. I'll need to question Melissa again, see if there's anything at all she can remember about Vincent's friends." She sighed. "One of them is his accomplice. We just need to figure out which one."

"Even though Rafe usually smells like smoke, he could've kicked the habit and still be involved. Or maybe Melissa didn't notice the smoke scent because everything happened so fast." He chewed for a moment, savoring the pizza. "I didn't know Vincent was on the rodeo circuit, I don't remember Melissa mentioning that. I guess if he was, it's logical he'd know the other guys. I still find it difficult to believe my ranch hands would stoop so low as to help kidnap a woman and child. Once we show Melissa their profile pictures, she might be able to narrow down the list of suspects."

"Except, he was wearing a ski mask." Her expression turned thoughtful. "I received a text from Bennett. He and Spike found the cabin where Vincent had held Melissa. There's no sign of Vincent or anyone else staying there, but we'll check it out again tomorrow just to be sure."

"Figures," he muttered.

"I keep going back to the desperation in Vincent's eyes as he held Melissa hostage to get Danny." She nibbled her garlic bread. "He must need the cash very badly. Since his goal was to sell Danny to the highest bidder, we may be able to use a decoy like a doll in a stroller to draw Vincent or his accomplice out of hiding."

"I'm willing to do whatever it takes," he assured her. "Are you planning to head to the police station tomorrow morning? I can set a doll in Danny's collapsible stroller, we have an extra one, and wander around the park for a while. If one of those guys is watching the place, and knows I'm there, they might make a move."

"Hold on, Cade." She lifted a hand in protest. "I need to talk this through with the upper brass first."

He nodded. "That's fine, but we need to take action and soon."

"I want this case wrapped up as much as you do." Ashley met his gaze. "But we need plenty of backup in place to prevent him from escaping, again."

She was right, so he nodded and sat back in his chair. "I know. Let me know when you've had a chance to formalize a plan. As I said, I'm willing to do whatever is necessary to draw Vincent and his accomplice out in the open." Smart to have additional cops on the scene to bring the guy down.

And to prevent him from planting his fist in Vincent's face.

No, he wouldn't hit the guy. Watching him being cuffed, arrested, and tossed in jail would have to suffice.

Ashley finished her meal first and began filling the sink with soapy water. He stuffed the last slice of pizza in his mouth and jumped up to join her.

When he could speak, he waved her away. "Sit down. It's not your job to clean up."

"I don't mind. I figure you may have more work to do outside, now that you don't have Danny to worry about."

In truth, it was strangely intimate to be here with Ashley without Danny. He didn't need her help anymore now that Melissa had Danny and they were both safe, yet she acted like they were a team. Partners, not just regarding the case, but in day-to-day life.

He could easily imagine coming home to Ashley after doing chores each day. And that image scared him. He didn't want to risk his heart again.

But it seemed his heart had a mind of its own.

Doing his best to ignore his complicated feelings, Cade forced himself to lighten things up. "I think the animals will be okay for the rest of the night. I can handle this." He nudged her away from the sink, taking over the task of washing dishes. "You should get some rest. Neither of us has gotten much sleep in the past few days."

"That's true. Although I have to admit, I'm surprised Vincent hasn't returned." Ashley frowned before adding, "I'll take Ozzy outside to make sure he isn't lurking nearby."

He tensed. "Be careful. We know he's armed and dangerous."

"I won't put Ozzy in harm's way." She pulled on her coat

then bent to secure the Lab's K-9 vest. "But I am a cop and it's my job to find and arrest the bad guys."

The way she put herself in danger to protect others was humbling. And frustrating. He appreciated her dedication to service, but he didn't like knowing she was heading out to protect him.

"Hold on. I'm going with you." He tossed the dishrag in the soapy water and then reached for his rawhide coat. "As you said, having backup is important."

She shot him an annoyed look then headed outside with Ozzy without waiting for him. He quickly followed, rifle in hand.

The crisp evening air held the scent of smoke from the fireplace. It reminded him of the cabin where Vincent had held Melissa captive. It had been cleared by Bennett, but Vincent could have been hiding out, waiting until later to use the place. Then again, if Vincent had any brain cells, which was debatable, he'd stay far away from the scene of the crime.

Cade had to admit, the idea to use a doll as a decoy to draw Vincent out of hiding had merit. If only he could figure out a way to make sure Vincent would know to look for him there. "Wait a minute." He turned to face Ashley. "You know the number of the disposable phone Vincent has been using, don't you?"

"Yes, and I already considered the possibility of sending him a message. But why would he trust a message saying the baby will be in the park? Unless he knew who it came from."

His spark of excitement faded. "I guess you're right."

"We'll think of something," Ashley assured him. The light from the barn illuminated her beautiful features and he couldn't help stepping closer.

But he caught himself. What was he doing? Kissing Ashley wasn't smart. Once she'd arrested Vincent and his accomplice, she'd move on with her work with the task force.

"Cade?" As if sensing his inner turmoil, she moved closer. "I want you to know—"

"We need to get inside," he interrupted.

She stared at him and, even in the darkness, he could see the wounded expression in her eyes. She turned away. "You're right. We do."

"Ashley, wait." He caught her hand, but she tugged it away. "I'm sorry. I like you. And I care about you. But I have to stay focused on Melissa and Danny. They need me."

"It's okay." The confusion that crossed her features belied her words. "I understand."

Did she? He wasn't sure he did, but he knew this was the only option. Their time together was almost over. Better for both of them to step back before they became even more emotionally involved.

He'd rather he and Ashley part as friends, not enemies.

Ashley couldn't shake her heavy heart. She didn't sleep well; even Ozzy noticed, lifting his head and touching her arm with his nose.

It wasn't rational to be upset with Cade's decision to focus on his family. Hadn't she been just as determined to prioritize her career? There were still five unsolved murders to investigate. She highly doubted she'd have time for a relationship with Cade.

She admired him, and yes, had been more attracted to him than she had been to Mike or any of the other guys she'd casually dated. But she wasn't looking to settle down.

By five thirty in the morning, she gave up any attempt to sleep. Moving silently, she took Ozzy outside then returned to make a pot of coffee.

In between analyzing her feelings for Cade, she'd tried

to come up with a way to draw Vincent out of hiding. She fed Ozzy and sat at the kitchen table with a cup of coffee, returning to the list of phone numbers that they'd pulled from Melissa's phone.

She knew now that Vincent had bought and used the disposable phone. It was early, but she put a call in to Isla about getting a call log from the burner.

To her surprise, Isla answered. "I hope I didn't wake you," Ashley said apologetically.

"No, I haven't been sleeping much, I keep waiting to hear from child protective services on Charisse, the foster baby I hope will be placed with me. What can I do for you?"

"I need to see the call log for the disposable phone used to lure Melissa away from the ranch house." She gave Isla the number. "I hate to pressure you, but I need this ASAP. We need to set a trap to lure Vincent out, so I need his accomplice's phone number."

"I'll get to it right away," Isla assured her. "Give me an hour or so, okay?"

"Thanks." She disconnected from the call, feeling satisfied to have a plan. Or at least, a partial plan.

Ozzy jumped to his feet, staring toward the bedrooms before she heard sounds of movement. "You have ears like a bat, Oz."

A minute later, Cade entered the kitchen, looking adorably rumpled. She wrapped both hands around her coffee mug to keep from reaching out to him.

"Good morning. Thanks for making coffee."

"You're welcome." Was that her husky voice? She needed to get a grip. "I hope I didn't wake you."

"You didn't. I slept like a rock for the first time since Danny was born." His mouth quirked in a smile as he filled his mug with coffee. "Yet I still miss seeing him."

"Understandable." She forced her gaze away, fearing

he'd see how attracted she was to him. "I figure we should head out early enough to reach the precinct around nine o'clock. I can make breakfast while you take care of the animals."

"You're sweet to offer, Ashley. Thank you." He propped his lean hip on the counter, eyeing her over the rim. "I have a good feeling about today. We're going to get Vincent, putting an end to this once and for all."

"I agree." She gestured to the computer. "I'm getting help with a phone number that I think we can use to send a message to draw Vincent out."

"Great." He nodded with satisfaction. "I better get to work."

He turned and poured his coffee into a reusable to-go cup, then shrugged into his coat. She watched as he slung his rifle over his shoulder and carried the coffee with him to the barn.

The house seemed empty without him, making her realize how quickly she'd become comfortable living there.

No more, she silently admonished. Hopefully, Cade was right about getting Vincent today.

She needed to take Ozzy to her own house. To get back into their normal routine. She glanced at her partner, who sat beside her. "Don't get too comfortable, we don't live here. This isn't our house, Oz."

His tail swished back and forth, as if in understanding.

When Cade returned she had breakfast ready. By the time they'd finished eating, Isla returned her call.

"An hour, huh?" Ashley teased.

"Sorry, I had to cut through some red tape. But you'll be interested to know that there are only two numbers that the disposable phone called." As Isla rattled them off, Ashley jotted them down.

"This is perfect." A surge of satisfaction hit hard. "One

is Melissa's number. The other has to be his accomplice's. You're the tech expert. Can you make a call so that it appears to be coming from a specific number?"

"Yes. But we should let Chase and Nora know about the plan," Isla cautioned. "They'll want to be included."

"I will." She met Cade's interested gaze as he stacked their dirty dishes in the sink. "We'll be at the precinct shortly. Thanks, Isla, you did awesome."

"I'm going to get the stroller." Cade dried his hands on a towel. "I don't have a doll handy, but I can stuff one of Danny's spare snowsuits with fabric to make it look like a baby."

"Good idea." She was excited that things were coming together. While Cade gathered what they needed, she contacted Nora. "We have a way to draw Vincent out of hiding. We'll need plenty of backup, though. I'll give you all the details once we arrive."

"I heard a bit from Isla, and I like the idea of drawing him out." Nora hesitated then said, "Not sure about using a civilian, though."

"Cade wants to be involved, and really, his presence will add authenticity. Vincent and his accomplice won't fall for this if they see me or another cop pushing the stroller. Hence why we need plenty of backup."

"I hear you, and I agree. We'll get things started on our end. See you soon." Nora disconnected from the call.

When Cade carried his homemade doll into the kitchen, she did a double-take. He'd found tan-colored fabric to use for the baby's face and drawn eyes on it. With the snowsuit stuffed with cloth, the hood tied around the head, she had to admit, the stuffed baby looked like Danny from afar.

"That's amazing," she said in awe.

"I figure your backup will assure this guy won't get close enough to notice it's fake."

"He won't. Let's go." She'd already taken Ozzy's supplies out to her SUV, knowing it wasn't likely she'd be back at the McNeal Four Ranch anytime soon.

Cade stored the collapsible umbrella stroller in the back seat, then set the stuffed-snowsuit pretend baby on top. She briefed him on what she knew of the plan so far on the drive to the precinct.

"I hope this works," he said with a sigh.

"Me, too." Ashley refused to consider the possibility of failure. The desperation on Vincent's face flashed in her mind. She firmly believed he'd jump at the chance to grab Danny.

Twenty minutes later, they were all huddled in the precinct conference room. Chase had covered the whiteboard notes he'd written about the Rocky Mountain Killer, to keep the information confidential. Cade sat at the end of the table, with the stroller and stuffed doll at his side. Everyone had looked at the fake Danny with approval.

"We need officers dressed in plain clothes," Nora said. "I'm concerned the K-9s will stand out, so you may need to leave them behind."

Ashley frowned. "I have a change of clothes in my car. Ozzy won't stand out too much if he doesn't have his vest on, and I can keep him off leash. He'll listen to me, no matter what."

Nora paused then nodded. "Okay, that's fine."

"I'll do the same with Spike," Bennett said.

"I think we need several other officers in plain clothes," Chase pointed out. "No offense, but Vincent will know Ashley, and possibly Bennett, on sight."

Ashley didn't want to be taken off the case, even though she knew he was right. "I can cover my head with a hat and wear large sunglasses to help hide my features. The good news is that the sun is out, so I won't look out of place."

"Okay, that should help." Chase turned toward Isla. "Are you ready to make contact?"

"Yes." Isla wore a headset as she worked the keyboard on her laptop computer. Ashley watched as she keyed in a text message then hit Send.

There was a moment of silence as they waited. "How long do you think it will take for a response?" Nora asked.

Isla's computer dinged. "The accomplice took the bait, believing the text about new information on where to find Danny as being from Vincent." She glanced up, her gaze questioning. "He's asking when and where?"

"The park in an hour," Nora said.

Ashley jumped to her feet so she could change out of her uniform. The trap had been set.

Now they needed to capture the rat.

FIFTEEN

Cade tugged the brim of his Stetson low on his head as he pushed the stroller with pretend Danny through Elk Valley Park. Being there reminded him of the day Melissa had been kidnapped. And how he'd been forced to flee the assailant to protect his nephew.

Not this time. No way was he running away. Just the opposite. The moment anyone tried to grab the stroller, he planned to take the attacker down. Provided one of the undercover cops didn't strike first.

He found himself hoping they wouldn't. Just the thought of the plan to sell Danny to the highest bidder made his blood boil. Muscles tense, his gaze darted from person to person, searching for Vincent or any young man showing an unusual interest in him and the stroller. They'd all agreed that the assailant, Vincent's partner, would be the one to show up. Unfortunately, they didn't know who to expect. One of their current suspects?

Or someone else?

The park was more crowded than he liked. The sunshine and warmer temps had brought everyone out to enjoy the day. He understood, as Wyoming winters were long, but today he'd have preferred less distractions.

He wore an earpiece connected to the police radio system. Occasionally, other officers would mention their location, but otherwise it was quiet.

Like the calm before the storm.

There was still ten minutes before the designated time-frame they'd given the assailant. The thought had been that the assailant would show up early, but so far, there was no sign of him. Cade pushed the stroller along a path that lined the woods, about twenty yards from the area where Melissa had been tied up. The hairs on the back of his neck tingled in warning.

Someone was behind him!

Loosening his grip on the stroller, he prepared to grab whoever was coming forward. Ashley's voice sounded in his ear. "Jogger on your left."

He gave a slight nod, figuring she was somewhere she could see him, and moved the stroller further to the right, to give the jogger room to pass. When the guy kept going without giving him or fake Danny a second look, he re-laxed.

"False alarm," he murmured.

"Stay alert," Ashley warned. "He's here, somewhere."

Cade nodded again to acknowledge her comment. As he continued along the path, he noticed a familiar woman sitting on a park bench next to man.

Elaine?

He couldn't make out who Elaine was with, the guy wore a cowboy hat and, with his head tipped downward, the wide brim shadowed his face. "Elaine is with someone," he whispered. "A guy. Can't see his face."

"I'll check them out," Ashley responded.

He slowed his pace, inwardly reeling. He'd assumed Elaine wasn't involved, but maybe she was! As he watched from the corner of his eye, Elaine reached up to wrap her arm around the cowboy's neck, drawing him in closer.

An act? Or for real? He didn't care who Elaine kissed unless the cowboy planned to spring forward and grab the stroller.

He slowed his pace, looking down at Danny as if he hadn't noticed them. *Come on, make your move*, he thought.

"I see her," Ashley said in his ear. "Stay alert."

Cade's muscles were so tense, he couldn't be any more alert. He continued walking past the kissing couple, fully expecting to be slammed in the back by the cowboy.

But nothing happened. It took all his willpower not to glance back over his shoulder to see what was going on.

"Elaine is kissing Mike Stucky," Ashley said in his ear. "He's on our suspect list, but he hasn't even glanced at you, Cade, or Danny. Bennett, would you keep an eye on the couple? I'm going to continue following Cade."

"I'm on them," a male voice said in his ear.

Walking slowly, as if he didn't have a care in the world, was difficult. Anyone who knew him would never believe he'd spend idle time in the middle of the morning walking with Danny.

But most criminals weren't super smart.

He paused and reached down to touch the pretend Danny, as if the baby was fussing. Talking to him, he allowed his voice to carry. "Hey, big guy, it's okay. It will be time to eat soon."

His plan was to walk the baby around, then find a place to sit where he could hold the stuffed snowsuit in his arms and pretend to give Danny a bottle. He'd felt certain the perp would strike while he was pushing the stroller, though, as it would be easier to grab it and knock him off balance to get away.

Striving for patience, he continued dawdling along the path. He passed an open area where there were more picnic tables, all of which were empty. Then the path curved, taking him past another wooded area. He scanned the trees, searching for any sign of an assailant, but the area was quiet.

Maybe too quiet.

Once again, the hairs on the back of his neck lifted in warning, even as a deep voice whispered harshly, "Stop or I'll shoot."

Cade stopped as ordered, hoping Ashley and a few of the other undercover officers would see him. "What do you want?"

"The kid." The voice didn't have Vincent's nasal quality to it, but sounded familiar. A moment later, he saw Stuart Berg move out from behind a tree, his gun leveled on Cade.

Cade knew he needed to act as if Danny were in the stroller. He tightened his grip on the handle as Stuart approached. It burned to know this young cowboy had worked as one of his ranch hands last summer. "No, I'm not giving you Danny."

"Then prepare to die," Stuart said calmly. The cold-as-ice expression in his eyes made Cade believe his threat.

"Police!" Ashley's sharp voice rang out. "Drop the gun!"

Stuart turned his weapon toward the sound of Ashley's voice. Fearing for her safety, Cade abruptly lifted the stroller and swung it with all his might, sending it sailing toward Stuart. The cowboy instinctively lifted his left arm to ward off the stroller as Ashley rushed forward.

"Drop your weapon!" Ashley shouted. Ozzy growled low in his throat, as if in warning. A sound Cade had never heard from the affectionate K-9. Then again, the dog was clearly protecting his handler.

To Cade's surprise, Stuart dropped the gun and raised his arms over his head. Then he glanced at the stroller that had fallen on its side, the fake Danny lying face up.

Stuart's expression reddened. "You tricked me!"

"Yep." Cade grinned as Ashley slapped handcuffs on Stuart's wrists. Then his smile faded. "Where's Vincent?"

Stuart averted his glare, clamping his lips shut.

Ashley recited the Miranda warning, telling Stuart he was under arrest for kidnapping, attempted kidnapping, and assault with a deadly weapon. When she finished, she asked, "Do you understand your rights?"

Stuart didn't respond.

"Answer me!" Ashley's authoritative tone had the cowboy looking up in surprise. "Do you understand your rights as I've described them to you?"

"Yes," he grudgingly admitted. "I understand."

"Good." Ashley pushed him forward, meeting Cade's eyes for a long moment. "You're headed straight to jail, Stuart. Let's see how you like being imprisoned against your will."

Cade picked up the stroller, tucking the fake Danny back inside before following Ashley and Stuart. Ozzy trotted alongside Ashley, his tail wagging, giving Cade the impression that the K-9 knew he'd done his part to get the bad guy. Seeing the dog made him smile.

Cade was relieved that their plan had worked, and that they had Stuart in custody. But he wouldn't rest easy until they had Vincent behind bars, too.

Ashley watched as Chase gently pushed Stuart into the back of a squad. She wanted to interrogate the guy, but knew they needed to be patient. Chase spoke to Bennett briefly, then waved to the officer behind the wheel of the vehicle to take Stuart Berg to the station.

"Good work, Hanson," Chase said. His praise warmed her heart.

"It was a team effort," she said honestly. "Without Isla's help, we wouldn't have gotten him."

"Yeah, but where's Vincent?" Cade demanded. Ironically, he didn't look at all silly pushing the stroller with the pretend Danny inside while asking. It was tempting to smile, despite the seriousness of the situation.

"I'm sure we'll convince Stuart to talk," Ashley said. "It may take some time, but I don't think he'll want to take the rap for this all alone."

"I'm heading back to the precinct," Chase said. "Go ahead with that interview, Hanson. I'm confident you'll get Stuart to cooperate."

"I wish I could be there when you question him," Cade said.

"You can't, but I promise to update you as soon as I have something. And you can wait in the precinct, if you like."

"I will." Cade glanced down at the stroller. "I'm glad our setup worked."

"Me, too."

"Will you unlock the SUV? I need to store these things inside."

"Sure." She hit the key fob for him. Cade took the fake Danny out and collapsed the stroller to store it in the back of her SUV. While he was doing that, Bennett Ford crossed over with his beagle, Spike.

"Do you need anything else from me?" Bennett glanced around as the undercover officers all headed back to the precinct. "By the way, the kissing couple claims they spent the past twenty four hours together, and had the hotel receipt to prove it. I don't think they're involved."

"That's something, I guess." And explained Elaine's absence from work and home.

Bennett offered a crooked smile. "Seems like you have everything under control, here. Not bad, rookie."

The rookie comment was teasing, and she found herself grinning in response. "Thanks. What were you and Chase discussing? New evidence on the Rocky Mountain Killer?"

Bennett's expression turned serious as he raked his hand

over his short cropped blond hair. "No new evidence yet, but I'm hoping to change that very soon. Chase just approved my plan. I'm heading back to my home state of Colorado to tail Naomi Carr-Cavanaugh for a few days. Considering how she was teased and humiliated by the guys in the Young Rancher's Club the night of the dance, I still think she has the biggest motive to lash out in revenge. I'm hoping to catch her in the act of doing something illegal."

Ashley lifted a brow. "She's eight months pregnant. You really think she's capable of killing five men in cold blood?"

His expression darkened. "She wasn't pregnant when she killed the first three victims." He waved an impatient hand to where Cade stood near her SUV. "Look what he's going through. Vincent tried to kidnap his own kid to sell him on the black market! If you ask me, anyone is capable of anything. I can easily see how a pregnant woman would kill two men."

She stared at the detective for a long moment, sensing for the second time now that his beliefs were rooted in some deep personal issue. What, she wasn't sure. "I understand your concern, Bennett. And I think tailing Naomi is a good idea. But one thing I learned in this case, is to keep an open mind. Preconceived notions can send you down the wrong path." She hesitated then added, "And to have faith in God's plan."

He frowned and glanced away. "In my mind, Naomi is guilty until proven innocent."

It was tempting to argue, but she knew many cops went into an investigation the same way. All suspects were considered possible until they were completely ruled out. "Be careful, Bennett. Remember there's an innocent baby involved."

"Yeah, and that's the worst part of the whole thing. That poor kid will likely grow up without either parent. And for what? Revenge over some ridiculous prank?" He shook his head, giving Spike the hand signal to come. Then he glanced at her. "I'm hitting the road. My gear is already in the back. Take care, Ashley."

"You, too." Troubled by his resolute opinion of their suspect, she offered a silent prayer for God to help guide him on the right path. And to protect Naomi's baby, the way He had protected Danny. She watched for a moment as Bennett pulled out of the parking lot and headed for the highway.

"Ashley?" Cade crossed over to join her. "Everything okay?" With the arrest, many of the park-goers had gathered around to gawk. But now they'd wandered off, leaving them alone. She hadn't seen Elaine or Mike, and figured they'd found somewhere more private to be together.

"It will be." She managed a smile. "I'm glad you're safe, that's the most important thing."

He searched her eyes for a moment. "How do you feel about seeing your ex-boyfriend kissing Elaine?"

The question surprised her. "I don't care about Mike. I suspect he'll cheat on her the way he did with me. You're the one who was once engaged to Elaine."

"Worst decision of my life," Cade said without hesitation. "I'm relieved she found someone else."

Her heart lightened at his words, even though she knew their time together was coming to a close. She was glad Cade was over Elaine. He deserved better.

Like her? She quickly pushed that thought aside. She'd been surprised at how little she'd felt seeing Mike and Elaine kissing each other. These past few days had shown her what a great guy Cade was, especially the way he'd cared for Danny.

For Cade, family was everything.

"Let's head back to the precinct." She decided to stay focused on the case. She reached down to pet Ozzy. "I'm anxious to question Stuart Berg about where we can find Vincent."

"Sounds good to me." Cade fell into step beside her. She took a moment to use the key fob to open the back hatch for Ozzy.

"Get in, boy." The dog jumped inside then let out a long, low growl. She instinctively stepped away, wondering if a snake had managed to get inside. March was generally too cold for snakes, but she didn't understand what had gotten Ozzy's back up.

Until she noticed Vincent was kneeling in the back seat, his gun trained on Ozzy.

She froze, silently praying the unstable man wouldn't shoot her K-9 partner.

"Get in, Officer," Vincent said in his nasal voice. "You're going to take me to the kid."

No, she wasn't, but she needed to find a way to get Ozzy out of the line of fire. The dog's attention was focused on the gunman, his low rumbling growls growing louder and louder. Ozzy couldn't obey a hand signal if he wasn't looking at her.

And Ozzy was too close to the barrel of Vincent's gun.

"Take me, Vincent." Cade stepped forward, lifting his hands and waving them to show he wasn't armed. "Leave Ashley and the dog here. They'll only slow you down. I'll take you to Danny."

Vincent's attention turned to Cade for a fraction of a second.

"Down, Oz!" Ashley shouted as she swiftly drew her weapon. On command, Ozzy jumped out of the SUV. Vincent's expression filled with rage and he turned to fire at Ozzy, thankfully missing her partner. She aimed her weapon and shot at him in response.

The glass of the rear passenger door shattered.

Vincent fell backward in the seat and, for a long moment, there was nothing but silence. Her heart pounded in her chest as Ozzy ran to her side, pressing himself against her. "Stay back, Cade."

"I will, but be careful."

"Stay, Oz," she said in a stern voice, unwilling to put him in danger. Still holding her service weapon in two hands, she moved toward the vehicle, half expecting Vincent was faking being injured and would vault upward to fire at her again.

"Vincent, you're under arrest for kidnapping and attempted murder of a police officer." She continued edging closer, trying to see inside the back seat. "Drop your weapon and put your hands where I can see them!"

Still no response and no movement. She reached the door with the shattered window and abruptly opened it.

Vincent was stretched out on the seat, blood staining the side of his head.

She took a moment to pick up the gun that had fallen from his grip and toss it aside. Then she holstered her weapon and reached for her radio to call it in.

"This is Unit 7. I'm still in the Elk Valley parking lot and have Vincent Orr here. He's suffering from a bullet wound. I need a bus."

"Ten-four, Unit 7. Bus and backup are on the way."

She stared down at Vincent, taking heart in the fact that he appeared to be breathing. The bullet had grazed his head, resulting in lots of blood. Head wounds bled a lot, and when she reached in to check his pulse, she could feel it beating fast beneath her fingertips. The impact of her bullet had knocked him unconscious, but she hadn't killed him.

At least, not yet.

She turned toward Ozzy and gave him the hand gesture to come. He ran to her, and she bent to draw him into her arms, pressing her face against his fur. After verifying he wasn't injured, she reluctantly let him go.

When Cade came up beside her, he put his arm around her as if sensing her distress. "He's still alive?"

"Yeah." Ozzy stayed close to her leg. She'd never fired her weapon at a perp, and wouldn't have done it now, if not for Vincent's attempt to shoot Ozzy.

"Good. I'd rather he rot in prison for the rest of his life," Cade said in a harsh tone.

"Me, too." She allowed herself a moment to lean against Cade, absorbing some of his strength, even as she dropped one hand to caress Ozzy's silky head. "Thanks for being a distraction. Your ruse worked." Then she frowned. "But you shouldn't have offered yourself as a target, Cade. He could have shot you."

"I was prepared to sacrifice myself to help take him down," Cade admitted. "Better me, than for him to get his hands on Melissa and Danny."

She shook her head, marveling at his courage, strength and determination. Cade was everything she admired in a man, especially his loyalty and dedication to his family. But he wasn't hers.

The wail of sirens, combined with pounding footsteps as Chase ran toward them had her stepping away from Cade. She might be dressed casually in jeans, sweater and winter coat from her undercover operation, but she was still on duty.

"I, uh, guess there's no need to rush over to interview Stuart about Vincent's whereabouts." She glanced at Cade as Chase approached. "I'll have someone drive you back to the ranch. From there, you can pick up Melissa and Danny from the safe house, too."

Cade frowned. "What about you?"

"I just shot a suspect." Thankfully, her voice didn't betray her nervousness. Looking back, she didn't see that she'd had any choice, but she could tell by the scowl on Chase's features that he wasn't happy. "I'll be tied up here for a while and likely placed on administrative leave."

"What happened?" Chase demanded.

She stepped forward, Ozzy remaining at her side. "I take full responsibility. It's my fault that the SUV was unlocked. And that I didn't notice Vincent sneaking inside."

"No, it's my fault," Cade said, stepping up to join her. "I'm the one who wanted to put the stroller away. I should have relocked the SUV, but didn't."

Chase's scowl deepened as he looked from Ashley to Cade and back to her. "You'd better start at the beginning."

"I'll explain everything," Ashley said. She handed her weapon to Chase, knowing it would need to be processed. "We can talk back at the precinct."

"I'm a witness," Cade said firmly. "You need to take my statement, as well."

Since he was right, she held her tongue. The ambulance pulled up alongside them. They all watched as the EMTs carefully removed Vincent from her back seat to place him on a stretcher. Then they swiftly wheeled him toward the ambulance.

"We need to make sure he doesn't escape once he wakes up," Chase muttered. "I need to assign a cop to ride along with him to the hospital, but not you, Hanson."

She nodded, understanding she would be on desk duty for the foreseeable future.

The danger was over. She could only hope and pray her career wasn't, too.

SIXTEEN

Cade worried about the despondent expression in Ashley's eyes. She hadn't done anything wrong. If she hadn't taken out Vincent, Ozzy would have been injured. Or killed.

This mess was his fault, and he wanted to be sure everyone within the Elk Valley Police Department knew it. He'd carelessly left the vehicle unlocked. If not for Ozzy's keen nose, the situation could have ended much worse.

"Let's get to the station," Chase said. "Nora is waiting for you, Ashley. We'll walk, your vehicle must stay here until it's been processed."

Cade winced, realizing the SUV was a crime scene.

"Come, Ozzy." Ashley's expression was grim as she followed Chase. Ozzy walked alongside her, looking up at her as if sensing she was upset. Cade hastened to catch up.

"It's going to be okay." He kept his voice low so Chase wouldn't hear. "I'll make sure they understand the role I played in this."

"I hope I'll be cleared of wrongdoing, but it's my fault, Cade. I'm the cop here. I should have anticipated Vincent would make another attempt to get to Danny." She sighed. "He was likely watching us the whole time."

"How though? He couldn't know we sent the text message to Berg, right?" Cade was trying to understand.

"Yeah, that part has me confused, too. Unless he followed Stuart here for some reason." She glanced at him. "Or followed us."

"I hope Vincent wakes up so that he can be interviewed," Cade muttered. "It would be nice to know exactly how this played out."

"Stuart Berg may know something. I'm sure Nora or one of the other cops will get the truth out of him."

"I'm sorry, Ashley." He felt awful about what happened. "I wish I'd locked the SUV."

"Hey, it's fine. Vincent would have attempted to get to us, no matter what. I guess it's better I was able to neutralize him here rather than somewhere more isolated." She shrugged and glanced at Ozzy as if reliving the near miss of his being hurt. "Besides, I believe Nora and Chase will be fair in how they handle this. Ozzy is a police officer, and I have a right to defend my partner."

He prayed the leadership would support her. When they reached the precinct, Ashley gestured to the lobby chair. "Wait there, Cade. They'll want to talk to us separately. Ozzy and I will be in Nora's office."

"Okay." He wouldn't argue police procedure. Dropping into the familiar chair, he scrubbed his hands over his face, taking heart in knowing the danger was over. Melissa and Danny were safe and could return to the ranch house where they belonged.

A stab of loneliness hit hard as he realized Ashley wouldn't be returning to the ranch house with him. How was it possible that he'd gotten emotionally involved with her in such a short period of time?

It didn't make sense. Yet the ache in his heart wouldn't go away.

"McNeal?" Chase gestured at him from the conference room. "I'd like to take your statement."

He sat at the conference table in the same spot as earlier, minus the stroller and fake Danny. He met Chase's gaze directly, hoping the FBI agent would be fair in his treatment of Ashley.

"Please describe what happened from your perspective," Chase said.

"I asked Ashley to unlock the SUV so I could put the stroller and pretend Danny inside. She was planning to drive me back to the precinct, then get an officer to take me home so I could head out to pick up Melissa and Danny while she stayed to interview Stuart Berg."

"Go on," Chase encouraged.

"I noticed she was speaking with Bennett, so I hung back until they were finished." He frowned, thinking back. He hadn't heard any movement from behind him when Vincent must have snuck into the car, but he hadn't been paying attention, either. He wished he had. "We spoke for few minutes about how she hoped to convince Stuart to give up Vincent, as there wasn't a reason for him to take the rap by himself. As we walked toward the SUV, she used her key fob to open the back hatch for Ozzy. He jumped in and instantly began to growl."

"Did you see Vincent inside?" Chase asked.

"Not right away. I was surprised to hear Ozzy growl, he rarely does." Although, the K-9 had growled when seeing Stuart in the park. The dog had great protective instincts. "Vincent held his gun on Ozzy, threatening to kill him if we didn't get in the car to take him to Danny. I stepped forward, asking him to take me instead. When Vincent glanced at me, Ashley ordered Ozzy to get down. Vincent fired at Ozzy, forcing Ashley to return fire."

"Vincent took a shot at Ozzy first?" Chase's gaze pierced his.

"Yes. I wouldn't lie about something so serious. Ashley didn't return fire until after he'd taken a shot at Ozzy. And, thankfully, missed hitting the dog."

Chase nodded and jotted notes. It occurred to him that the FBI agent was involved in this for two reasons. One, because the Feds often assisted with investigating officer-involved shootings, especially with smaller police departments like this. And because Ashley was a member of his task force. He obviously had a vested interest in her conduct.

"Ashley only did what was necessary," he repeated.

Chase finished his note. "Anything else?"

Cade thought back, but couldn't come up with anything to add. "I am curious about why Vincent was there. He wouldn't have known about the fake text from his phone."

"Maybe he did know, and set his accomplice up to take the fall." Chase shrugged and stood. "We'll find out more from Stuart Berg. Thanks for giving your statement on the officer-involved shooting incident. I've asked Ed Gerund to bring your sister and nephew here to pick you up. He'll drive all of you back to the ranch."

"I'd rather wait for Ashley." He followed Chase into the lobby. As much as he wanted to have Melissa and Danny home, he didn't want to leave without speaking to Ashley.

"She's going to be here a while." Chase gestured toward the doorway. "No point in waiting around. Besides, Gerund just pulled in."

Cade stared helplessly at the police chief's closed office door. Realizing he didn't have much of a choice, he turned to head outside.

Maybe this was for the best. He couldn't possibly have fallen in love in the span of a few days. He needed to focus on the ranch. He was behind on so many chores that he could work from sunup to sundown for a week straight without getting caught up.

"Cade!" Melissa slid out of the front seat of the squad car, rushed over to throw her arms around him. "I'm so glad to see you. Is it really over?"

"Yes. Vincent is wounded and at the hospital, and they have his accomplice, Stuart Berg, in custody, too. You and Danny are safe."

"I'm so glad." She hugged him hard then stepped back, glancing around in surprise. "Where's Ashley?"

"Inside." He decided not to go into detail. "She'll be busy for a bit. We'll head back to the ranch now. It will be nice for things to return to normal."

Melissa cocked her head. "I've seen the way you look at her, Cade. You care about her. A lot."

"I made a mistake with Elaine, remember?" He scowled. "You should have told me about the argument you had with her at the Rusty Spoke. And you should know I'd always choose family over anyone else."

"I did know that, which is why I didn't bother you with the petty argument." Melissa turned to look at Danny in the back seat of the squad. "Danny is the most important part of my life. But, keep in mind, you need to be happy, too. I hate hearing you compare the two women. Ashley is the polar opposite of Elaine. I've only been with her briefly, but it's obvious she fits in with us far better than Elaine ever could. You deserve to be happy, Cade."

"Ready to go?" Gerund asked, clearly getting impatient.

"Yes." Cade opened the front door for Melissa then climbed into the back with Danny.

The three of them were family. But as Officer Ed Gerund drove them to the ranch, Melissa's comment about how well Ashley fit in with their family reverberated through his mind.

Deep down, he secretly agreed with his sister's assessment. The only problem he had was what to do about it.

Ashley spent several hours at the precinct going through the sequence of events until Nora was satisfied. She'd learned that Stuart had spilled his guts upon hearing Vincent was also in custody. No surprise, really. It didn't take much for criminals to flip on each other. Turns out Stuart had verified the location of Danny being at the park with Vincent. Vincent had known it was a trap and had sent Stuart in to make the grab anyway, likely hoping he'd get the chance to force them at gunpoint to take him to Danny.

Chase offered to drive her and Ozzy home, and the way he'd filled her in on Stuart's confession made her feel like a full-fledged member of the team.

"According to Stuart, Vincent had found a site on the dark web where babies could be sold for big money," Chase said. "He had gambling debts and was looking to make enough to pay those off while keeping a nice chunk of change for himself."

"Horrible," she murmured.

"Yeah, I'm going to get the cybercrime arm of the FBI to dig into that site a bit more." Chase frowned. "We have a division on human trafficking, too, that will be very interested in that information. That site needs to get shut down and fast."

"I'm glad. It's awful to think other children may have been sold in that way." Chase pulled into her drive and shifted the vehicle into Park. She reached for the door handle. "Thanks for the ride."

"Don't forget you're on leave until the investigation is complete," he said as she slid out the passenger door. He opened the back hatch to let Ozzy out, too. Dash's tail wagged as if saying goodbye to his fellow teammate. As a credit to his training, Ozzy instantly came to sit at her side.

"I know." She hesitated then said, "But I can sit in on the task force team meetings, right?"

"Yeah, that's fine. You just can't do anything in the field

until you're cleared. Hopefully, it won't take too long until you're back at it."

"Okay. Thanks again." She led Ozzy inside her small house. It had been three days since she'd been there. Three days that seemed like three months.

Being alone had never bothered her; as an only child, she'd spent many days and nights by herself. But the silence seemed to close around her. Even with Ozzy there, the place felt empty.

She missed Cade and Danny. More than she'd thought possible.

Grabbing a microwave meal from the freezer, she tossed it in the zapper then fed Ozzy while it was cooking. She talked to her partner, more so to keep the empty feeling at bay. It helped a little.

Yet, that night, sleep eluded her. By morning, she was more on edge than ever. Ozzy stayed close to her side, as if sensing she wasn't herself. She let him out and then fed him his breakfast. Her bread was stale, so she made toast and sipped coffee, staring blankly outside.

At some point, she needed to call her father, to let him know what had happened. But not yet. She didn't trust her dad not to try to pull strings with Chase or Nora to get her back on full duty.

Because the job was everything to him.

But not to her.

The realization brought her up short. She loved her job, and being part of the task force, but she didn't want to be like her father.

She would never allow the job to be more important than family. Remembering how Cade had offered himself up to Vincent to protect Melissa and Danny had proven he would never allow anything, like his ranch, to be more important than his family, either. She admired that about him and was even more determined not to make the same mistakes her father had.

The question remained. Where did she fit in Cade's life? If at all?

Unfortunately, she had no way to get to the McNeal Four Ranch to talk to him. Her SUV was still being processed by the crime scene techs. She could try to find a ride, but didn't know who to call.

Bennett had left town yesterday. She was ashamed to realize she didn't have many close friends she could ask for help. Another side effect of being too focused on her career.

Well, enough of that. She had acquaintances who could become friends.

Pulling out her phone, she called Isla. "Isla? It's Ashley. I, uh, need a favor."

"Of course," Isla agreed. "I'm sure you heard about Cowgirl and want to come in to help search for clues."

"Wait. What are you talking about?" Ashley paced the small living space. Ozzy was stretched out on the floor, watching her with his dark eyes. "What happened to Cowgirl?"

"Someone took her early this morning. Liana had her outside in the training center when she thought she heard gunfire. She turned to look for a shooter then called for backup on her phone. After she finished talking to the dispatcher, Cowgirl was gone. Liana saw a man in black running away, disappearing into the woods." Isla sniffled as if she were crying. "Cowgirl loves everyone, so it's not a surprise that she didn't bark or growl. Liana feels terrible and is taking full responsibility for the dognapping."

"Poor Liana," Ashley felt terrible, as if she were somehow responsible since getting Cowgirl was her idea. What if the dognapper treated the labradoodle badly? She swallowed hard, trying not to panic. "I don't understand, why would anyone kidnap Cowgirl? She's trained as an emotional support dog. It's hard to imagine someone would steal her to use her services elsewhere."

"I know. It doesn't make any sense. The worst thing about it is that Cowgirl hasn't been chipped yet. No collar and no chip will make it harder to find her."

That was even worse. "That's awful. But, Isla, I'm on leave, so I don't think I'll be allowed to work the case."

"Oh, I forgot about that. Hey, Chase just waked in. I have to go." Isla disconnected from the call without saying anything more.

Ashley tucked her phone away. Distressed by the news of Cowgirl being taken, she took a moment to send up a prayer for the labradoodle's safety and that she would be returned unharmed.

With everything going on, this was hardly the time to ask for a ride to the ranch. She sat looking down at Ozzy, who rested his face in her lap.

"You're such a good boy," she murmured. "Guess I'll have to clean today. And do laundry." The routine household tasks would not help keep her mind from ruminating over her confusing feelings for Cade.

With her first load of laundry in, she began cleaning the kitchen. Ozzy let out a soft woof and went over to stand by the door. She frowned. "What is it?"

The black Lab's tail wagged back and forth as he stood expectantly in front of the door. A sharp knock had her crossing over to peer through the window.

Cade?

Concern for Melissa and Danny had her wrenching open the door. "What is it? Are Melissa and Danny okay?"

A smile tugged at the corner of his mouth. "They're fine, but it's nice that you care enough to ask. May I come in?"

"Uh, sure." She opened the door wider so he could enter

her small kitchen. Ozzy greeted him like a long-lost friend. He removed his Stetson then bent to pet the dog.

"Yes, buddy, I missed you, too," Cade crooned.

Now that Cade was standing there, Ashley was at a loss for words. All the things she'd planned to say were locked in her tight throat.

"Ashley." He set his cowboy hat on the table and then stepped closer. "I wanted to see if you were okay. And to ask if you would like to have dinner with us tonight."

"Dinner?" Her voice came out a high squeaky sound that should have been embarrassing.

"Yes, dinner. Well, we could do lunch and dinner." His smile widened. "To be honest, I was thinking you could spend the day with us. Maybe see what it's like to work with the livestock."

She managed to find her voice. "Is this your way of making sure I don't mope around because I'm on leave for shooting Vincent?"

Cade's intense green eyes locked on hers. "That's part of it, but the truth is I miss you. I miss having you and Ozzy at the ranch. The place isn't the same without you."

Her heart squeezed. "Oh, Cade, I've missed you and Danny, too."

He took another step closer and slowly drew her into his arms. "I'm glad to hear that because I think I'm falling in love with you, Officer Ashley Hanson."

"Really?" Now her heart soared. She wrapped her arms around his lean waist. "Oh, Cade, I thought it was just me. I think I'm falling in love with you, too."

"That's a relief." He grinned then bent to capture her mouth with his. His kiss curled her toes, and she would have happily spent the rest of the day kissing him, but Ozzy butted his head against her thigh.

"Go away, Ozzy," she murmured, resting her head in the hollow of Cade's chest.

"He sure wants to be a part of your embrace," Cade drawled.

With a chuckle, she reached down to stroke Ozzy's head. "He wants to be with both of us."

"I would like that very much." Cade gave her another heated kiss, then pulled his head back to look down at her. "I know your job is important to you, but I'm hoping we can find a way to make our divergent schedules work."

"My job isn't as important as you and Melissa and Danny," she corrected. "I tried to find someone to take me to your ranch so I could tell you that."

"I'm glad," he murmured. "It was Melissa's comment about how I deserve to be happy that got to me. Despite the danger, I always felt as if you were my partner. Willing to help in any way. I was upset over Melissa being gone but, oddly enough, I was also happy with you, too. Your support was invaluable." His expression turned serious. "And I wanted to help you, as well. We were good together, Ashley. That's as important as my family. All of my family." He kissed her again. "Including you and Ozzy. And maybe a new puppy if you'll help me train him. I've been thinking we need another ranch dog to help with the cattle. You're the best dog expert I know."

"I'd like that very much." She was touched that he'd come all this way to ask her to spend the day with him. She was content to take things one day at a time.

"Ozzy and I would love to come to the ranch for lunch and dinner."

"Great." He finally loosened his arms to step back. "What can I do to help you pack some stuff?"

"Pack what stuff?" She stared at him in confusion.

"You know, horseback riding and work gear. Warmer

clothes and boots." He grinned. "You look great, but you'll want to wear older clothes to work in the barn."

The way he was folding her into his life was endearing and a little alarming. "I haven't been on a horse in a long time," she warned.

His grin widened. "No worries, it's like riding a bike. You'll be fine." His gaze softened. "I love you, Ashley. I can't wait to share all aspects of the ranch life with you."

Her eyes misted with emotion. "I love you, too."

When he pulled her into another embrace, she didn't resist. Being held in his arms was like coming home to a place she belonged.

With Ozzy, and the promise of a new puppy, too.

* * * * *

*If you enjoyed Ashley's story, don't miss Bennett's story
next! Check out* Her Duty Bound Defender *and
the rest of the Mountain Country K-9 Unit series!*

*Available only from Love Inspired Suspense.
Discover more at LoveInspired.com*

Dear Reader,

I hope you enjoyed *Baby Protection Mission*, the first book in our Mountain Country K-9 Unit series. I'm truly blessed to have been able to work on this series with a great group of authors. I hope you get a chance to read every book. You won't be disappointed.

As always, the stars of our books are the dogs themselves! I had fun writing about Ozzy and the rest of the K-9s, especially showcasing each dog's individual personality.

I adore hearing from my readers!

I can be found through

my website at https://www.laurascottbooks.com,

via Facebook at https://www.facebook.com/Laura-ScottBooks,

Instagram at https://www.instagram.com/laurascottbooks/,

and Twitter https://twitter.com/laurascottbooks.

Also, take a moment to sign up for my monthly newsletter. It's the best way to learn about my new book releases. All subscribers receive a free novella not available for purchase on any platform.

Until next time,
Laura Scott